W9-AHK-822

DISCARD

WHO IS JESSE FLOOD?

WHO IS JESSE FLOOD?

malachy doyle

BLOOMSBURY

Published by Bloomsbury, New York and London
Distributed to the trade by St. Martin's Press

Library of Congress Cataloging-in-Publication Data
Doyle, Malachy.
Who is Jesse Flood? / Malachy Doyle. p.cm.
Summary: Striving to cope with the arguments of his parents and his feelings of
not belonging, fourteen-year-old Jesse Flood struggles to find his place in a small
town in Northern Ireland.
ISBN 1-58234-776-X (hardcover: alk. paper)
[1. Emotional problems—Fiction. 2. Family problems—Fiction. 3. Identity—
Fiction. 4. Northern Ireland—Fiction.] I. Title.
PZ7.D775 Wh 2002
[Fic]—ds21
2002019065

ISBN: 1-58234-776-X

First U.S. Edition 2002

1 3 5 7 9 10 8 6 4 2

Bloomsbury USA Children's Books
175 Fifth Avenue
New York, New York 10010

for Raphael

part one

Off the Rails

Jesse Flood – Age 14

You go down Shore Road, past the quarry, under the bridge and head out towards the Red Harbour. You climb up on to the railway line, stopping off maybe at the hut where you once found all those pictures of naked women plastered to the walls. You check no one's about, and then you steam up to the tunnel. There'll be a train in ten minutes, so you don't hang about. You venture into the darkness, keeping to the hard gravel at the side of the track. No torch, of course. Only wimps carry torches.

You feel your way along the wall, your hands slipping on a hundred years of dirt and grime, till you get to the first recess. Every so often there's a narrow one cut into the wall, like an upright coffin. For the railway workers, probably, in case they're taken by surprise. They must have been small, though, the first

9

railmen, because you can only just about squeeze in, with your head pressing hard against the top.

So you're pushing into the gap, as tall and straight as you can manage so none of your bony bits are sticking out into the path of the train, and then you hang out your head and listen. For the clattering on the rails, for the ear-splitting whistle. Trains aren't famous for coming early, of course, but with your sort of luck, anything's possible.

No sign, yet, but you know one's on the way. You know the timetable back to front and any minute now the train's definitely coming. There wouldn't be much point doing all this, otherwise.

You carry on, further into the blackness. Stopping off at each recess for a quick check, and then on again. You walk, you stumble into the disappearing light, a hundred metres or so till you've reached the gap right in the middle. The mid-point where there's no light from either end because of the curve. You force yourself up against the wall again, pressing yourself even further back than before, because this time it's for real, this time it's just you and the train.

It's cold and dark and you know your mum'll go mad when she sees the state of your clothes, black and stinking. You'll make up some sort of a story, of course, but it won't stop her nagging.

Your dad'll tell her to pack it in, woman, it's giving him a sore head. And once they've started they'll go on and on at each other all evening, trading insults over the mumbling television, till you manage to distract their attention by drawing the blame back on to yourself. Because that's the way it goes.

Oh, drop it, Jesse. Drop it from your mind. You didn't come into the tunnel to think about them, them and their never-ending bickering. You came in here to escape all that stuff.

It's a sort of hell, really, down here in the pitch black. Wedged into your railman coffin, with nothing to see, nothing to hear. No one to bother you, mind. No one to tell you what to do, what not to do. No one to draw you into their petty arguments. Yes, it's a sort of hell, but it suits you.

So you wait, breathing as quietly as you can, and then you hear the whistle. Three blasts, to say it's on the way, through the Brown Hills, passing the Red Harbour, thundering down the line towards the tunnel. Louder and louder, closer and closer, thundering, thundering, thundering . . .

Your brain tells you there's got to be enough room in there, pressed up hard against the wall – they couldn't afford to lose too many railmen, just the fat ones maybe – but your body doesn't really believe it. Your body's worried about all those bony bits, sticking out just a little too far because they only made the hole for dwarf labour. Are people so much taller now? Can a teenage boy really be that much bigger than one of the old railway workers? Come to think of it, aren't trains different now too? For one thing, they don't belch out tons of smoke like they used to – the smoke and soot that's still in there, clinging to the walls, to your clothes, your hands, your face, your lungs. But aren't they wider now, trains? Wouldn't they push up closer to the side of the tunnel?

Nearer and nearer, louder and louder, and suddenly there's a blinding brightness, searing into your eyes. You forgot they turn on the lights to go through. The driver'll see you, recognize you. Quickly, you turn your face to the wall. Straight into a mouthful of muck.

You pull away and for some reason you're screaming now, screaming with fear. You push in again, in case the back of your head gets whopped by the train. You're yelling and the whistle blows a second time, it

12

never blows a second time, and the train's already inside the tunnel and the sound is amplified a thousand times, forced down towards you, and suddenly it hits your eardrums.

The train's upon you and the noise is deafening and you can't breathe and it drowns your yelling and you don't really know if you're actually hearing anything anyway now that your eardrums have exploded. Maybe it's all just in your imagination and you're not even really here and you're just in bed and it's just a dream and if you open your eyes everything'll be OK.

You open your eyes and everything's not OK. There's a filthy black wall slap bang in front of you and you're pushing and pushing, up against it. The noise is horrendous, all around you, and you're shaking, shaking, losing control of your body. It wants to fall, it really wants to fall, but you're forcing it, forcing it upright. Because if you slip you'll go under, slip you'll go under, slip you'll go under the wheels of the train.

And you're thinking maybe this wasn't such a good idea after all. You're thinking maybe there are better ways to get the constant sound of parental argument out of your head. Slightly more clever ways to get yourself a cheap thrill, to break the unremitting tedium of small town life. All this you're thinking, in the few seconds it takes for the train to pass.

Maybe that's what they mean about seeing your whole life flashing past at the moment of death. Is this the moment of death? Because the basic underlying fear, the ultimate incredible kick, the sheer bloody terror of the whole thing, is the sure and certain knowledge that you're maybe about to die. You really think you might die.

And then it's gone. The train's gone. An aftershock, as the foul-smelling air rushes past you, and then a terrible, ringing silence. You open your eyes, turn to look where it was, whether it was, and there's a great black nothingness, all around. Nothing but darkness and silence, and you wonder if you really are dead. If you really are in a coffin. If you're really, maybe, in hell.

The tension drains from your body, the fear that made you rigid slips away, and you can't stand up a second longer. You buckle almost to your knees, but for some reason your stomach doesn't drop with you. No, it climbs into your throat, fills your throat and you retch. Retch till your breakfast splatters your boots, till the tea and cornflakes form a soggy, smelly mass on the scuffed black leather.

And then slowly, slowly, the smell revives you. Slowly, the stinking aroma brings you round, prods you into action. Yes, slowly, ever so slowly, you sort your head out and realize you've got to get moving, got to get moving, got to get out of that hell-hole.

So you walk, you stumble, one foot in front of the other, knees like jelly, to the end of the tunnel. As fast as your messed-up brain allows, basically. Because you know that very soon, if he hasn't done it already, the driver'll stop in the station and send a man back to check if there really was someone there. To check if he saw what he thought he saw or whether he just imagined it.

And if by any chance he didn't see you (but he must have, in the glare of the headlights, or why would he have blown the whistle inside the tunnel?), then there'll be another train coming the opposite way any minute now, and one's enough for today, thank you very much.

The daylight's opening up ahead and you can make out the curve of the coastline now, the lighthouse up on the headland. Then, as you step out into the blinding sun, there it is, Greywater. Boring little seaside town, the place you're supposed to have delighted in calling home for the past fourteen interminable years, there it is, stretching out in front of you. Aimless, brainless, purposeless Greywater, staring out to sea like a washed-up sailor.

You raise a finger to it, to all the tedious old farts who live there, and then you laugh. Hell and Greywater, in the space of five minutes! You throw yourself on to the grass and roll down the bank, turning it black as soot behind you. You pick yourself up when you get to the path and you're still laughing, hysterical now, the tears dripping down your face.

And then you run. Run to the quarry. Run, hide, before they catch you.

Hey, you did it, Jesse Flood! You did it!

One more way to find excitement at the arse end of the Universe.

Ranting, Raging

Typical. Just bloody typical. First day I go to school in ages, and Frostbite decides to clamp down on school uniform. You'd think he'd be glad to see me. You'd think he'd be pleased that I chose to turn up, for once.

Clap his arm around my shoulder, break the habit of a lifetime, grin a mighty grin, and say, 'Young Jesse Flood, it's great to have you back!'

But oh no! It's make-an-example day. Let-them-know-who's-in-charge day. Petty bloody officiousness, that's all it is. I mean, is it any wonder I've given up on all this crap?

'OUT! OUT! OUT!'

Everyone who's wearing jeans, the wrong top, jewellery, Docs, dyed hair, anyone with the slightest ounce of individuality. Anyone with half a brain, basically. Anyone who dares to think for themselves, who can't bear to act like a complete robot for thirteen years while they pack your head full of stuff that's no use for nothing. Only so you can pass the odd exam to make their precious statistics look halfway good by the time you leave, and then they dump you in some mindless job, or on the scrapheap, like Dad.

So you end up the sort of mindless jerk who doesn't ever, ever, EVER question the system. The sort of dullbrain who thinks it's fine that four per cent of the people have ninety-five per cent of the wealth or whatever. Who thinks it's perfectly OK that multi-national corporations exploit the poor, strip the earth's natural resources, fire bloody great holes through the ozone layer. I mean, I may be only fourteen but I know what I'm talking about. Oh yes, I watch the news. I read the Sunday papers. I know what's going on.

They're cutting down the Ladies up on One Tree Hill, that's what they're doing. They're clearing all the rainforests, killing off the animals, poisoning the water, and for what? Destroying all our planet, and for what? Yes, they're destroying the planet that my generation, MY generation, has a responsibility to look after and pass on to OUR children. And for the sake of what, may I ask? For the sake of what are they raping our world? For the sake of lining the pockets of a few very rich men, that's what!

So what about that? What have you got to say about that, Mr Oh-so-wonderful Businessman?

So there we are in the corridor, while Frostbite, the bloodless professor, is in the next-door classroom, turfing out half of that lot as well. People are unscrewing their nose studs, spitting on tissues to wash off their make-up, desperately composing their lies, creating their alibis.

'I'm sorry, sir. My mum put it in the wash.'

'Terribly sorry, sir. My younger brother took mine by mistake.'

'I'm deeply apologetic, your Highness. They were nowhere to be found.'

'Please may I kiss your precious cotton socks, mein Führer, and swear that I shall never again allow my hair to grow even an inch. And gosh, you'll never guess, but I've an appointment at the hairdresser this very afternoon!'

Oh, wake up! Wake up, you children. Shake off the chains of your mobile phones and your teenage crush-es and get in touch with what's really going on here.

What people like him are doing to OUR world!

And then Frostbite reaches me. Meek, mild-mannered me. And I'm so sick to the stomach of all their sucking-up, all their crawling up his tight backside. So sick of him, even more, that something happens. Something majorly weird. The words I'm thinking, the thoughts that usually stay deep in my subconscious, the sort of things I wouldn't ever even dream of actually saying, certainly not to the abominable Frostbite, rise up and out and into the air.

'Well, to tell you the truth,' I find myself saying, looking him straight between the eyes. 'I hadn't actually planned to come in today. I was going to spend it in the Town Library . . .' I carry on, ignoring the looks of horror on the faces of my classmates, some of whom had been in exactly the same situation but had no intention of saying so, '. . . but it was closed so I thought I might as well come up here and see what was happening.'

Gasps from all around. Frostbite goes puce.

'I BEG your pardon?'

Help! I'm having some sort of a personality bypass. Some sort of emotional freak-out, right here and now, in front of everyone. But now I've started I can't seem to stop.

'As I said, sir, I wasn't coming in,' I repeat slowly, paraphrasing myself this time in case he's too thick to understand. 'I was planning to do some revision in the Town Library, for my upcoming examinations, you know, but . . . '

It's true. I don't know how I'm actually saying it, why I'm actually saying it, but it's true. The past few weeks they've only being going over the same old stuff in class, for the ones who didn't listen the first time. It's boring, terminally boring, so I've taken to spending my time down in the library, where they've got lots of little quiet spaces where you can get on with your work without any interference. I can get much more done there than I would in school, so what's he got to moan about?

But then Frostbite explodes. 'This is insolence, boy! Downright insolence! How DARE you? How DARE you talk to me like that! How DARE you come in here dressed like a tramp and then have the sheer unadulterated cheek to tell me that you had no intention to set foot in my school in the first place? How DARE you tell me that you consider the Town Library a more suitable educational establishment for

21

fulfilling your puny academic aspirations. The town dump, more like!'

And he looks round at the others, hoping to raise a laugh at my expense. And fails, miserably.

'Take it easy, sir,' I say, trying to calm him down. I mean, he can be quite amusing sometimes, old Frostbite, in a frigid sort of a way, when you're not the one he's venting his spleen on. But if the full force of his sarcastic splutter is targeted at you, then all you want is for the ground to open up beneath you.

Someone up at the end of the line, amused by my cheek, amazed at my answering back, almost as amazed as I am, in fact, tries unsuccessfully to suppress a giggle. Frostbite casts them an evil glance.

'TAKE IT EASY!' he yells, parroting me. 'Where on earth do you children get such revolting phraseology? If you'd only spend more time at your studies, as I'm forever trying to drum into you, and less time watching cheap television, you wouldn't be coming out with all these inane mid-Atlantic clichés. You wouldn't be losing all respect for authority. You . . .'

He's back on his favourite hobby-horse, but then he remembers me.

'And you, Jesse Flood! Just look at you!' he splutters. 'For one thing, you look as if you haven't washed your hair for weeks!'

He's right, of course. I heard somewhere that shampoo's bad for you, and most of it's tested on animals anyway, and that if you leave your hair alone, nature takes over. After a few weeks the natural oils get back to doing what they're designed to do, and Bob's your uncle. Or something like that. Mind you, maybe I should have washed it after that tunnel business.

'Your shoes are FILTHY!' he yells. He's got a point there, too. 'There isn't a suspicion of school uniform anywhere on your disgusting body . . .'

'Steady on,' I say. 'I mean, there's no need to get personal.'

More horrified sniggers up and down the line. Another killer glance from Frostbite.

I don't quite know what's going on here, as a matter of fact. I was always as terrified of this guy as the next wimp. In fact, probably even more so. He'd come into class, whenever one of the teachers failed to turn up, and a deathly hush would descend on the place. Heads down, avoid eye contact, don't get singled out.

But somehow, somewhere, something's changed. It's not as if I ever had any respect for him – he never did anything to earn it – but there was certainly fear. Fear of his power, his anger, his capacity to humiliate you, to make you feel worthless, to serve it up double by getting in touch with your parents and trying to get them to do the same. But all that's gone now. I don't know when or why or for how long but something's changed inside me, and I won't put up with all this crap any more. Not in the mood I'm in today, anyway.

'The insolence! The utter INSOLENCE!' says Frostbite, fit to burst. And then his voice drops to a chilling whisper. 'I hope, Jesse Flood,' he says, spitting out my name like it's some sort of swear word, 'that when you are in a position of influence and responsibility, a position that demands RESPECT, not that that's ever likely the way you're going on, but if you do, if you ever do, I hope, I sincerely hope, that you encounter this DISGRACEFUL level of OUT-RAGEOUS insolence from the people you are supposed to be leading. Then, only then, will you know what it's like for me!'

Oh dear. Poor Frosty. I'm supposed to feel sorry

for you now, am I?

'Look,' I hear myself saying, glancing up and down the line and then back at the Boss. It's like I'm standing outside myself, watching. Waiting. 'You've got it all wrong, here,' I carry on. 'If I was in your position I'd much rather be told the truth, however unpleasant, than a pack of lies. If I had any influence, I'd want to use it to help people to think for themselves, instead of just turning them into mindless morons who only tell me what I want to hear, rather than what they really believe. Rather than what's fair and just and honest and . . .'

That's done it, of course. Now I've really gone and done it. Not only have I made inevitable my immediate expulsion, but by drawing his attention to the highly dubious nature of everyone else's excuses, I've alienated myself from just about everybody else in my year.

But I mean, it's sickening, all those fairy tales about little brothers and washing machines, all that crawling. Why can't they just come out with the truth, like me, and make old Frostbite face up to the fact that it's ridiculous in this day and age trying to force young adults into uniform, trying to force us to all look the same, think the same. Those days are over, mate. Look at America. Look at France, Australia, Germany. I mean, why does this stupid country always lag decades behind anywhere with any respect for the rights of young people? It's stupid, stupid, stupid!

'GET OUT!' he yells, marching me down the corridor. He's following in my footsteps, close enough for me to feel the frozen fumes of his stinking breath on the back of my neck, even through all that grease and tunnel-muck.

And it's perfectly obvious, to me anyway, that what he really wants to do is to grab hold of me, to shake the last remaining brain cells out of my insolent skull, if only he could get away with it. But he can't, of course. He can't, because everyone else would see him. He can't, because he's desperately trying to preserve the last of his authority, the remaining shreds of his dignity, in front of the others.

'Take your things and leave my school, NOW, Jesse Flood!' he yells, shoving me out the door. 'And DON'T COME BACK!'

Me and my big mouth. I've really gone and done it now.

Soppy Love Songs

It's Saturday morning. I ease open the door. There's no sign of Dad.

'Who's that?' says Mum, blearily. 'Oh hi, Jesse.'

I climb in beside her, snuggle warm.

Until five, ten, twenty minutes later she says, 'Would you be a love and nip down and make us a cup of tea?'

I'd rather stay in the warm, her warm, but I want to please her, I want to make her happy, so I clamber back out again. Pad down the stairs. The cats come rushing out of the kitchen when I open the door, do a quick circuit of the hall and then dash back in.

'Come on, then, you guys.' I laugh, filling the kettle before going into the utility room and reaching up for a new tin of cat food.

Fork the smelly gunk into their bowls, keeping down the feeling of nausea it always gives me, and they're pushing and shoving, like they haven't eaten for days. Chuck in a handful of biscuits and leave them to sort it out between them. Then I make two mugs of tea and carry them back up to Mum's room.

'Thanks, love,' she says, sitting up. 'There's nothing like a cup of tea in bed to make you feel like a new man.'

Whatever that means. And then she laughs.

And that's the closest we come to discussing Dad.

I don't ask where he is. It's obvious, really. Sleeping off a heavy night, somewhere. The usual Friday night thing. He goes down to the pub at seven thirty and that's the last we see of him till Saturday afternoon, when he arrives back in time to watch the sport on telly. He's helping his friends, the ones that do have jobs, spend their earnings, so he says. They've got so much spare cash rattling around in their pockets, that lot, they need a bit of help to lighten the load. So he says.

It's annoying but it's also not annoying. Him disappearing, I mean. Because even though it's just one more time when he's not around when he should be, even though it's just one more piece of evidence that he's a no-good waste of space, as Mum never misses the opportunity to remind him, at least it lets her have a lie in, a rest at the end of a hard working week, without any grief. And it gives me a chance to spend some time with her. Some 'quality' time, as they say.

'So, how's my handsome Jesse?' she says, ruffling my hair.

'Oh, OK,' I answer, only mildly embarrassed. I mean, it's not as though there's anyone to see.

But I don't tell her how I really am. I don't tell her about the tunnel. About Frostbite. About not having a school to go to any more.

I'd rather just lie here, in her warmth. Wallowing in one of her rare good moods. Sitting up, every now and again, to let the hot air from the tea steam round my face.

'How about you, Mum?' I ask. 'You OK?'

'Oh, I'll survive,' she says. 'Work's been tough this week, with Sandra off sick, but somebody's got to do it. And it pays the rent.'

'Any plans for the weekend?' I ask her, getting the question in before she does. Just keeping the conversation ticking over, really. Keeping it off anything difficult.

'Oh, a bit of gardening. A bit of reading. Tidy the house. Wash the clothes. The usual sort of thing. You?'

'I don't know, Mum,' I say. 'Not a lot.'

'What a hectic life you lead, Jesse Flood,' she says, laughing, before snuggling back down under the covers again.

And then, after a while, we get up and have breakfast together, just me and her, with the radio warbling on in the background. Soppy love songs.

I loved those mornings. Those quiet, easy mornings, when it was just me and her.

No rush. No hassle. Just me and her.

One Tree Hill

Here's what I do when things are bad. One or more of these.

Walk – round the headland, up to the reservoir, out to the Island, anywhere, basically. Just walk, one foot in front of the other, letting my mind go blank. If it's raining, all the better. It goes with the mood.

Music – up to my room and blast out some metal. On the headphones if I think it's going to annoy anyone. Not on the headphones, if I think they deserve to be annoyed.

Books – escape into another world. Replace the here and now with someone else's. The longer, the rougher, the wilder, the better.

Or stories – I've a head full of them. All because of my mum. She'd sit on the side of my bed, when I was younger, and weave these fantasies. I never really knew if she was remembering them, from things she'd been told when she was a child, or whether she was making them up. A bit of both, probably. But somehow they've found their way into my head now, too, and I wouldn't be able to get rid of them, even if I wanted to. I carry them around in my brain, and I never actually tell them to anyone, I never actually pass them on, like you're supposed to with stories, but they're in there anyway, twisting and turning, growing and changing, and it's as though they've become a part of my life.

They've a habit of taking over when the outside world starts going all fuzzy on me. And then it's not like they're make-believe any more. It's like they're real. It's like I'm a character inside them, living out my mother's dreams, living out my own. It's like the people from my real life find a form inside the stories. I don't know why.

And they're not the same stories my mum used to tell, any more. They're different now. They're about me. They're about the things I do, the things I don't do. The things that make me smile, the things that make me mad.

Like when they're cutting down the rainforests, poisoning our planet. Like when they're chopping down the Ladies up on One Tree Hill.

*   *   *

High on a hill stood three tall trees. On a moonlit night there was music, and three Green Ladies danced. People feared the Green Ladies, for they knew they were the spirits of the trees, and no one dared go near but the farmer who owned the land.

Once a year, on Midsummer Eve, he'd climb to the top of the hill to lay a handful of late primroses at the foot of each one. The leaves rustled and the sun shone and he always made sure he was safe indoors before sunset.

It was a rich farm and the old man often said to his three sons, Dan, Stan and Patrick, 'Our luck lies in those trees, boys. When I'm gone, be sure and don't forget to treat them with respect.'

They listened and they heard and they were like every young man there's ever been. They thought they knew better than their father, they thought the new ways were better than the old, and they didn't take a blind bit of notice of the old fellow's advice. Except for young Patrick.

When the father died the farm was divided into three. Dan, the oldest, took the biggest and best fields, including the hill with the three trees on. And

33

the pastures below were so good that he didn't bother with the hill. Not at first, anyway.

And Stan, the middle brother, took everything else that was worth having, so that all young Patrick was left with was a strip of poor rough ground at the foot of the hill. But he didn't seem to mind. No, he set to work, did Patrick, and he whistled as he worked. And he was always indoors before the sun went down, so the Three Green Ladies could dance unseen.

One evening his brothers came to see him. Their larger farms weren't doing so well and they were jealous, for on Patrick's land the small patch of barley swayed in the breeze, fruit hung heavy from his apple tree, vegetables grew fat, the chickens laid all year round and his cows gave pint after pint of rich creamy milk.

'Who helps you in your work, little brother?' asked Dan. 'For you can't be doing all this by yourself. I've heard tell,' he said, giving Patrick the evil eye, 'that there's music and dancing from somewhere over this way, long after a hard-working farmer should be in his bed.'

But Patrick kept his silence.

'Didn't I see you up by the trees as we came?' said Stan. 'What were you doing, little brother?'

'I was doing as Father said,' said Patrick. 'Showing respect for the Three Green Ladies. It's Midsummer Eve.'

But the other two looked at him as if he was mad. They hadn't the slightest memory of their father's warning.

'That hill's mine, little brother,' cried Dan. 'Don't let me see you up there again! And as for those trees, I need wood for my new barn so I'll be cutting one of them down tomorrow. Who's going to help me?'

Middle brother Stan didn't offer, pretending he had to go to market instead. He was never one for doing more work than he had to, was Stan.

And Patrick? Oh, Patrick kept his silence as usual. He knew there was no way he could stop Dan doing what he wanted, for the eldest brother had a fierce temper. But there was a great sadness on Patrick at the prospect of what was about to happen, for he loved those trees more than almost anything in the world.

The next day Dan came with a horse and cart and up he went, up the hill to the three trees. When he laid his axe to the first of them it screamed, and his horse ran off in alarm.

The wind howled and the other trees lashed their branches in anger, but Dan ignored all the signs and kept on chopping till the tree was about to fall. She leaned one way, leaned another, until Dan was mesmerized. He knew he had to run, but he couldn't decide which way was safe, and while he stood, rooted to the spot, the First Green Lady came crashing down on top of him.

By and by the men came and took away the dead man and the dead tree. Now only two Green Ladies danced by the light of the moon, and all Dan got for his efforts was a coffin.

Stan, the middle brother, then took both farms for himself, leaving Patrick still working his small strip of land. But he never complained, did Patrick. He worked hard, and he whistled as he worked, and he was always indoors before the sun went down, so the Two Green Ladies could dance unseen.

And he never forgot what his father had told him. He never forgot to bring primroses up the hill every Midsummer Eve.

The big farms still didn't prosper, for Stan was lazy, very lazy. One day he came over to see how Patrick was getting on, and saw him up by the two trees.

'Get away from that hill, little brother, for it's mine now!' he yelled from below. 'I'm going to put a strong fence all around, to stop your cows eating my grass. And I'll be cutting down one of those trees to make it!'

The Green Ladies must have heard Stan, for that night there was no music, just the crying of a thousand leaves. And in his farmhouse Patrick, too, was sad.

The next morning Stan came with an axe and the two trees shuddered. He kept a close eye on the wind to make sure the tree he was taking out didn't fall on him, like it had on his older brother. But the Second Green Lady screamed as he chopped, and young Patrick watched from the lane below as she twisted in agony at the very last minute and came crashing down on Stan.

The people came and took away the second dead brother and the second dead tree and, like Dan before him, the only thing Stan got out of it was a coffin.

Patrick now owned all the land, but he didn't move into either of the rich farmhouses, preferring to stay on in his little cottage, as near as he could to One Tree Hill.

He was a busy man, and a rich one too, but he

always remembered to leave a bunch of late primroses by the roots of the lone tree on Midsummer Eve. And sometimes, only sometimes, on a moonlit night he would hear a sad little tune and know that the last Green Lady was quietly dancing.

The whole farm prospered now that Patrick was in charge. Great fields of barley swayed in the breeze, orchards hung heavy with fruit, vegetables grew fat, chickens laid aplenty and his herd of cows gave rich creamy milk.

And in time Patrick found himself a loving wife and had three pretty girls. And the girls had no fear of the Green Lady, not one bit. In fact, they became friends with her, the Last Green Lady up on One Tree Hill, and danced around her every day.

And that's my story. It's all about respect, see. Respect for nature. For the future and the past.

Me and the
Opposite Sex

It's not as though I really WANT to be so different to everyone else. It's not as though I always want to be on the outside, looking in. That's just how it is.

Take girls for example. Even now, I still can't figure them out. Maybe it comes from not having much in the way of Green Ladies in my life, not even having a sister, but I never know how to talk to them, really. And I still can't quite sort out what you're supposed to do about them. All that boy-girl stuff. I mean, I'm not dumb. I watch TV, I read books, I know what goes on. But I can't quite relate it to my own life, somehow.

Jesse Flood – Age 13¾

Take the day I was coming home on the train. It was when I was still going to school most of the time. Before I had that major run-in with Frostbite.

Anyway, we were just approaching the tunnel, the one I was on about earlier.

They're supposed to turn the lights on inside the train, as well as outside, when they're going through. So nobody falls over if they're walking down the corridor. So little kids don't scream and big kids don't mess about. Yeah, they're supposed to turn them on, all right, but half the time they never do.

So it all goes dark and there's this sudden rush of noise, like there always is when you hit the tunnel, and then loud, really loud over the top of everything, this voice cuts through the darkness, 'SOPHIE CAMERON LOVES JESSE FLOOD!'

Who, me? You gotta be joking! I squirm, I look all around for somewhere to escape from all the prying eyes that'll be focused entirely on me as soon as we're back in the light. All those laughing, sneering, mocking eyes.

Fumbling about in my bag, I pull out a book, any book, and pretend to be engrossed in it. Embarrassed as hell, though. Even more embarrassed as we come out into the light and I realize the book's upside-down.

Anyway, this hot flush of a blush rises up from my socks to my scalp and I think I'm going to die, I'm that mortified. I think I'm going to overheat, to melt into my seat, drip on to the floor and pour under the doors, on to the line.

Till the train pulls into the station and I'm first off, up the hill and away.

I know who it was, too, mocking me. I recognized the voice. It was Beca Douglas. She and that Sophie Cameron, the one she was on about 'loving' me, for God's sake, they always sit together. They go to that Posh Girl's School up on the Malone Road. Come to think of it, wasn't that them up at the end of the carriage when I got on?

I used to spend a lot of time with Beca, when we were younger. Except she was Rebecca in those days. Plain old-fashioned Rebecca. She lives in the big house further up the hill from us. They've got a golden retriever and a grandfather clock and a granny who lives with them called DawDaw, except she's dead now. I used to love it there – we'd play hide-and-seek up in the attic, me and Rebecca. Her mum used to make us German biscuits, and sometimes DawDaw would try and teach me how to play Go, the world's most intelligent game, according to her, but I never could get the hang of it.

I think she thought I was a bit stupid, did DawDaw. Somewhat less than the world's most intelligent friend for her beloved granddaughter. Or is it grandawdaw? Anyway, I stopped going there when I was about nine. It all tailed off somehow. I don't quite know why.

And Sophie Cameron? I've seen her about, of course. But she's one of the Yacht Club types. Or her family are, anyway. She lives in another big house, up at the very top of town. Her dad's an architect or something. And I'd have to admit it, just between you and me, if you're twisting my arm, like, there's no denying she's pretty. With that long blonde hair, down to her waist, and a smile that lights you up just to see it. God, I sound like one of those stupid love songs my mum listens to.

I try to ignore it, of course. I try to pretend it doesn't happen. But it does.

And you know who Sophie reminds me of? Yellow Lily. The girl in the story, another of the ones my mum used to tell me. In fact, that's what I call Sophie sometimes, in my head – Yellow Lily. It's my secret name for her. When I'm watching her, out of the corner of my eye. When I'm thinking of her, in my day dreams, my night dreams.

But it only makes it worse   Sophic bcing pretty, I mean. It only makes it worse when I hear people yelling things about her fancying me. I mean, if it was someonc that made me heave just to look at her, like Sarah Gillespie, for example, well it wouldn't be so bad, now would it? I'd still be embarrassed, chronically embarrassed probably, if everybody was turning, staring at me, laughing at me. But it's even worse when it's Sophie Cameron.

Because I've never really admitted it before, even to myself. But I really do want her to like me.

How ridiculous! I mean, how dumb can you get! Here's me, ugly as sin. Here's me, who never even talks to girls, wanting the prettiest one in the whole town to show an interest in me.

Get real, son. Just get real.

But why can't they leave me alone? Why do they have to taunt me, all these people, just because I'm different, just because I don't hang round with a gang, don't play sports, don't show an interest in girls? Just because I'm not like everyone else.

I mean, why does everyone have to be the same?

I mean, why do they have to make fun of me? Even

people like Beca Douglas, people with no harm in them at all.

You know, it's a funny thing, being different. You wear this invisible badge everywhere you go that says, 'I'm an outsider, because I want to be.' I suppose it's not so invisible, really, because it's in your clothes, your hair, the look on your face. Most of the time people see it, and let you get on with it. They keep out of your way because you're not part of the way they live. They don't bother with you because you don't affect them. Don't bother you, unless you push it.

I'm different, that's all. I just want to live my life my own way. I don't want to rub it in anyone's face. Don't want to have some sort of a big show-down about it. Unless it's Frostbite, and I'm having an emotional freak-out.

So you get away with it, generally. Being an outsider. But just occasionally they get it into their heads to try and drag you, kicking and screaming into their world. As if they need proof that their way is the right one. They think they're doing you a favour, when really they're trying to get you to do them one. To tell them they're OK. That they've got it right and you've got it wrong.

And then you get the twisted ones. The ones that pick on you in all the meanest ways because they feel threatened – threatened by anything different. They're just plain evil, and you're first in the line of fire because you stand out from the crowd. I don't want to talk about that lot, but I've learnt how to deal with them, sort of. How to keep out of their way, at least.

But what nobody ever questions is whether it's true. Whether the invisible badge that says, 'I'm an outsider, because I want to be,' is a star of truth or a bundle of lies. Because does anybody really want to be an outsider? Is it really worth it? Or is it just a position you've been forced into, you've forced yourself into?

Sometimes I'd love to fit in, see. Sometimes there's nothing I'd like more than just to be the same as everyone else. It'd make life so much easier. I'd have more friends. I wouldn't stand out like a sore thumb all the time. So sometimes I try, I really do try to play the game their way. I'm just not very good at it.

And anyway, the badge doesn't really protect you, not like the Sheriff's badge in those old cowboy movies always deflects the bad guy's bullets. You build up this big hard shell around you, so things don't get to you, but they do. It does this time, anyway.

It gets to me because even though I never talk to Beca Douglas any more – I'm not a part of her life now – I don't see why she'd want to mock me, to humiliate me. I don't see why she'd want to draw everyone's attention to the fact that I'm unlovable. I mean, we used to be friends, me and her.

Just because I'm different now. Just because every other boy my age seems to be obsessed with getting off with girls, and I'm not. Just because I don't know how to talk to the opposite sex. Just because . . . just because of everything, it doesn't mean she, they, have to make fun of me.

Me and the Opposite
Sex, Part Two

It's not that I can't talk to them, girls that is, it's just that I never seem to know what I'm supposed to say. What I'm supposed to do about it.

For a while I used to go to Youth Club. It's a pretty rubbishy Youth Club, to tell you the truth, but it was something to do. Because there's not a lot else round here, like I said. And maybe it's some sort of instinct thing, some sort of preservation of the species thing, but there's this naggy little voice somewhere deep down inside me that tells me I've got to do what I can to prevent myself dying of boredom before I've even left school.

So we'd trudge off to this whoopy doopy Youth Club to play table tennis and pool and listen to music and there'd always be a Responsible Parent about to make sure there was no mucking about, no snogging.

Jesse Flood – Age 13

I remember one time, about a year ago it was, all the boys were crowded round this stupid toy slide projector thing somebody'd brought in, laughing and such like. I didn't generally bother about them much, that lot, except to thrash them all at table tennis, but this time they came up to me and said, 'Jesse, Jesse, look in here. Look in here, Jesse.' And I ignored them.

And they said, 'Jesse, Jesse, look in here. Naked women, Jesse!'

And I ignored them. What would I want to look at naked women for?

They went off to annoy someone else but they came back a few minutes later and they said, 'Only joking, Jesse. It's not naked women, it's Tom and Jerry. Look, Jesse. It's really funny.'

So I took it off them, the stupid projector thing, just to shut them up, like, and I looked into it and I couldn't see anything.

'Hold it closer!' they said, so I pushed it into the socket of my eye, trying to focus in on the cartoon capers. Still nothing.

'Turn it, Jesse! Turn it!' they said, so I pushed

it and I turned it, and I turned it and I pushed it, but there was nothing there, nothing but darkness. No cat, no mouse, no naked women, nothing. There I was, pushing this stupid bit of plastic as hard as I could, pressing it into my eye socket, round and round till it hurt, and I still couldn't see a damn thing.

I pushed it back to them and suddenly they were all pointing at me and laughing. I sloped off to the toilet, then, to stop them looking at me, and to see what they were laughing at. And when I stared in the mirror what did I see but this great black ring all around my eye, a great ring of black ink from that ridiculous projector thing.

I tried washing it off but it only made it worse. I couldn't find any soap, and water just smeared the ink all over my face. I banged out of the toilet, furious with them, even more furious with myself for being so ridiculous. Intending to go straight home, but there they were, them and a whole lot more, all standing round waiting to get another good look. All laughing their legs off.

And I couldn't decide what it was about me that they were laughing at the most, which they thought was the stupidest. The fact that I'd fallen for the oldest trick in the book, or the fact that I preferred kiddy cartoons to naked women.

I never really did fit in, see.

Me and the Opposite Sex, Part Three

Girls. I just don't seem to think about them like everyone else does. I could cope with them as friends, maybe, but the trouble is there's so much pressure to take it to another level. It's like, you're not allowed to just enjoy each other's company, you have to be going out together or something.

Take Gina Kennedy, for example. I never bothered with her much at primary school, she's a year or two younger than me, so she was just one of those snotty-nosed little kids you never really notice. But then she started coming to Youth Club with a gang of other girls, and there was something about her. Something that made me notice her, her glossy red hair that she used to wear in silly pig tails when we were at school together but now swished around her shoulders, catching the light as she walked. Her high-pitched laugh that used to annoy the hell out of me in the playground but now, even though it wasn't a whole lot different, made me smile just to hear it, made me want to be with her, to share in her happiness. Something about her clothes, too. The shape of her.

Jesse Flood – Age 13¼

'Hi, Gina. Do you want a game of table tennis?' I said one night, a couple of months after that stupid projector business.

She'd arrived early, without the usual giggle of friends. There was only me and her there, so I thought I might as well. I mean, there wasn't anything else to do.

We played, and it was fun. More fun than I'd thought it'd be. We started playing most nights then, because she's better at it than any of the other girls, and she's not annoying, like all those stupid boys I was telling you about. She'd arrive early, before everyone else, and we'd play.

And instead of just playing to win, trying to get it over with as quick as possible, seeing if I could take every game without losing a single point, which is what I usually try to do, I found I was actually enjoying it. It was actually a 'game', a way to have a good time, rather than just a contest. A fun way to pass the time, rather than just the one way I had of proving I was good at something.

At one point, early on, when it became obvious that I was a whole lot better than her, I even offered to let her start ten points up, so she'd have more chance of keeping up with me. So she'd have some sort of chance of actually maybe even beating me sometimes. I couldn't believe my generosity. I don't know what got into me. It's not something I'd normally even dream of doing.

But she turned me down! 'No thanks, Jesse,' she said, smiling. 'I'd rather just play. I'm not all that bothered who wins, you know.'

It made me think, that did. Think about table tennis. Think about Gina, too.

So we'd be laughing and chatting, me and her. The games'd go on much longer than they usually do, and sometimes we'd even stay talking together for a while after we'd finished. It didn't feel like I was actually talking to a girl, though – it couldn't have or I'd have just clammed up, because that's the effect they always have on me.

So there we'd be, over by the music, chatting away.

Not for so long that anyone'd notice, hopefully, but long enough. Until she went off with her friends and some kid would come up and challenge me to a high-pressure game. Someone who wanted to prove to his mates that he could get at least five points off Jesse Flood, the ping-pong king. Time to call back up the killer instinct. Time to show the little squirts what's what.

But it was good, being with Gina. It made the whole evening good. It even made me feel good about myself.

Until Charlie Ferguson, ladies man despite the skinhead haircut and the ever-present acne, sidled up to me one night and said, 'You fancy her, don't you?'

'Who?' I said, a bit shocked that he was even there beside me, never mind what he was actually saying. I never really talked to Charlie, see. He'd only recently moved into the new estate at the top of town. His family had come over from Scotland, when the new fish factory opened, up the road in Castletown, but already he was one of the lads, one of the gang, and I'm not. Not and never will be.

One for the girls he was, too. And I'm not that either. Not and never will be.

'Gina Kennedy,' he said. 'It's obvious you fancy her. Just look at you.'

It wasn't obvious to me. It wasn't obvious at all.

'Ask her out,' he said.

No way.

'Go on,' he said. 'Ask her out. Anyone can see you're dying to.'

Was I? I didn't think so.

I went home early and tried to escape into a book. Fantasy, folktale, science fiction. Somewhere where there's a whole world of difference. It's the best way I know to hide from reality, from other people's expectations.

But this time it didn't work. I kept having to read the same page, the same paragraph over and over. My mind kept shutting off in mid-sentence, shutting off from the carefully composed alternative realities in front of me. Returning to the wit and wisdom of Charlie the pain Ferguson.

'Ask her out. I know you're dying to.'

I didn't want to ask Gina out. I just wanted to talk, to play table tennis. I wanted her to be a friend, I suppose. Just a friend. I didn't really want to think of her as a girl, because if I thought of her as a girl I'd have to clam up, draw back. I certainly didn't want to 'fancy' her, whatever that meant.

No, I didn't want all that stupid boy-girl Charlie Ferguson-type stuff to get in the way of what we'd already got. To lower the tone of our friendship. What business was it of Charlie's, anyway? What right had he to come nosing in? I bet he was only doing it to see me make a fool of myself. I'd been watching him. I'd seen what he was like.

It would spoil it. Spoil what me and Gina had together. And anyway, I didn't know how to do it. I didn't want to do it.

But then my mind turned. Slowly, my mind turned. Maybe Charlie wasn't just trying to humiliate me. Maybe he was right. Maybe that's what's supposed to happen, now I'm thirteen, I thought. Maybe that's what Gina's waiting for, I thought. Maybe that's what she wants, she just doesn't want to have to make the first move, she just needs to know I feel the same way.

And maybe I did feel the same way. Maybe I really did 'fancy' her, I was just too scared to do anything about it.

I needed someone to talk to about it, but there wasn't anyone. No one who'd understand. If only there was someone who'd listen, someone who'd care enough to understand. There was Mum, yeah. But she was slipping away. Too caught up in her own stuff.

'How?' I asked Charlie, the next night, over by the speakers. Where the music would drown out our conversation, so no one else could hear it.

'How what?' he yelled.

'How do I ask her out?' I hissed. 'You know, Gina.'

'Don't you even know that yet, Jesse Flood?' he said, looking at me as though I was some sort of worm, just crawled out of a hole. 'You really are sad.'

I shook my head, and he took pity on me.

'Just say, "Can I walk you home?" or something.'

What would I want to walk her home for? She lived right on the other side of town and I lived just round the corner.

But I considered it, nevertheless. It seemed a bit pointless, but somehow it felt like I had no choice. Now that I'd gone to Charlie Ferguson asking advice, I'd no alternative but to go ahead. Otherwise I knew he'd go blabbing to all the lads about what a wimp I was and I'd never hear the end of it.

I didn't play table tennis with Gina that night. The

whole thing had put me in a really bad mood. I thrashed a few of the younger kids, mercilessly, and then I hung around the speakers, choosing all the music I like and no one else does, blasting the metal at top volume just to annoy everyone. Till one of the Responsible Parents came over, eyeballed me, and asked me to turn it down.

There was nothing else to do, then, but watch Gina out of the corner of my eye, wait for her to get ready to leave.

The trouble was she was with all her friends, all her annoying, giggly, girly, friends. Next thing they were putting on their coats, and I knew if I didn't do it now I never would. So I plucked up every bit of courage I possessed, sidled up to her, and muttered, 'Would you like me to go home with you, Gina?'

'You what?' she said, taken by surprise. I knew I hadn't said it properly. I knew I'd got the words wrong. And I knew I'd probably mumbled it so quietly there's no way she could have heard me right, anyway. But I didn't want all the other girls to hear. I couldn't BEAR them to hear.

But you promised yourself, Jesse Flood! You PROMISED yourself!

'I SAID, CAN I WALK YOU HOME?'

I knew I'd got it right this time, but the tone was all wrong. It came out all loud, aggressive, unfriendly. The other girls burst into fits of giggles, Responsible Adult turned down the music and started walking towards us, everyone in the room turned to look, and I felt my skin turn red from head to toe.

There was a moment's hesitation from Gina, a split second only as she caught my eye and looked away. And then, 'Sorry, Jesse,' she said, blushing too. 'I told Kate and Maddy I was going back with them.'

And she turned and went.

And I watched her beautiful red hair disappear out the door.

And I never played table tennis with her again.

More Trouble Than They're Worth

More embarrassments. Getting a Valentine's card three years in a row from Sarah Gillespie. Sarah Gillespie! Yuk! I mean I know I'm not exactly God's gift to women, but I'm not that desperate. And how long does it take someone to get the message, anyway?

More embarrassments. Finding out that Charlie Ferguson was going out with Gina Kennedy. How could she? How COULD she?

Jesse Flood – Age 13$\frac{1}{2}$

And the Youth Club trip to Castletown! It still makes me cringe, just to think of it.

The table tennis team were invited to Castletown Youth Club for a match. February, it was. Two or three months after the Gina thing. We didn't actually have a team, because we never played anyone, but we sorted out six players and off we went in the church minibus, with Responsible Parent driving. Not mine, of course. Not Charlie Ferguson's, either. I don't think ours would qualify, somehow.

Castletown's about five times as big as Greywater, and the kids from there look down on us like we're from the scrag end of the universe. We are, of course, but we're never going to admit that to them. So they've got all these facilities we can only dream of. A real live secondary school – wow! A mayor – whoopee!

Mind you, they have got a leisure centre. Squash courts. And a proper purpose-built Youth Club. Not like our knackered old shed.

So in we walked, into their oh-so-impressive purpose-built Youth Club, and everything stopped, even the music. They all turned to stare at us, like we were this rare and endangered species, *Homunculus greywaterus* or something. Smalltown hicks.

They gave us a free Coke each. Gosh, such generosity. To build up our strength, I suppose. Poor undernourished country cousins.

And then we played the match. It was serious stuff. No keeping the score yourself. It was all official umpires and strict rules. No hiding the ball in your hand before you served. Touch the table and you lose the point. And I thought I was strict!

It turned out we were playing their second team – we weren't considered good enough for their first. At the start, when we worked out who was on their team, it looked like it was going to be a walkover. We'd stuff them, no problem.

But, would you believe it, we were thrashed. Beaten every game. It was awful. In the very first game Charlie Ferguson got stuffed by this eight-year-old. An eight-year-old! He was tiny! And then they put some girl on against me. Call that a girl? I bet she was on steroids or something. And imagine my utter humiliation when she beat me, 21-16, 21-16. God, I thought I'd die!

I mean, what's the point of living if you can't even beat a girl at table tennis? I always thought it was the one thing I was good at, but no. I'm a failure, even at that.

But that's not the embarrassment I wanted to tell you about. I mean, that was bad enough, but this is even worse.

After the match I was hanging about, waiting for the bus to take us back to Greywater, when Charlie Ferguson grabbed hold of me.

'Hey, Jesse,' he said. 'Come with us!'

I should have known he'd only cause me trouble, after the Gina Kennedy business, but I didn't have time to think. He pulled me out the door and next thing me, him and two of the Castletown girls were off down the road to the harbour.

'Hi, Jesse!' said one of them, linking her arm in mine and smirking up at me. I'd never seen her before in my life. I mean, we hadn't even been introduced.

'Uh,' I muttered, not best pleased at the developing situation.

'I'm Tracey,' she said, not at all put off by my unpleasantness. Smiling her broadest, most winning smile.

'Uh.' Play the neanderthal. Don't make eye contact.

Mind you, it was obvious that Charlie and the other girl were playing an altogether different game. Quite clearly they had no intention of wasting time on the preliminaries. He was already wrapped around her, like a bread roll round a hot dog, and you could see it was going to take a JCB to prise them apart.

'Hey, look. Isn't that a lesser spotted black backed gull?' I said, feigning an acute interest in ornithology. Well I had to do something to escape the attentions of the dreaded Tracey.

But no one appeared to share my enthusiasm for our feathered friends.

'Charlie! Don't you think we should be getting back?' I said, as soon as I spotted him coming up for air.

No answer.

'Charlie. The bus'll go without us!'

Still no answer.

This went on for ages, me getting more and more embarrassed, Tracey getting more and more bored, and Charlie and his new-found girl getting more and more steamy. Until eventually the two of them managed to peel themselves apart long enough for me to insist on returning and for Tracey to make it clear to her friend in frantic sign language that she wasn't getting anywhere with frigid Jesse and that she wanted to go back to the Club.

I assumed she thought I was terminally boring – Charlie Ferguson might be a hot dog, but I quite clearly couldn't cut the mustard, French or otherwise. But it turned out she was made of sterner stuff. Maybe she was desperate or something. Because as soon as we got back Tracey led us into a side room, someone switched off the lights, and suddenly she was all over me. Yuk! She was pawing me, nosing around my face, and next thing she planted her mouth slap bang on top of mine. Eek! It was all slobbery wet and this horrible tongue thing was trying to poke around in my dental cavities. And as if that wasn't bad enough, close up I discovered that her breath stank of chewing gum – chewing gum and apples. I've always HATED chewing gum and apples.

Next thing the door flies open, the lights go on, and there's Responsible Castletown Youth Leader, breathing fire and brimstone.

'WHAT ON EARTH is going on in here? Charles Ferguson! Jesse Flood! Take your hands off those girls, leave my Club this minute and DON'T COME BACK!'

We sloped off to find the others, our tails firmly tucked between our legs, only to find to our disgust that my warning to Charlie down by the harbour had been correct. Everyone else had disappeared!

Responsible Greywater Parent had sent out search parties, no doubt, failed to find us, been worried about getting back later than expected, and gone!

There was nothing for it but to walk home. The last train went at nine, there were no buses, and we hadn't any money anyway. Neither of us dared ring our parents and ask them to come and pick us up, because it'd only mean explaining what had happened. Better to just get back under our own steam, and hope they didn't notice we were late. Late and very wet.

Because it was nine miles, it was pouring with rain, and I'd a massive hole in my shoe. Massive by the time we'd walked a few miles, anyway.

At least there was no chance of getting lost, as it was simply a matter of following the road that ran beside the railway line, that ran beside the sea. So we knew the way, no problem, but it was pitch dark. No street lights in this part of the world. Whenever we heard a car coming we took it in turns to face it, to stick out a thumb and smile inanely. But it never worked. It obviously wasn't our night. Well, it wasn't mine anyway.

Some of the cars slowed down, but we must have seemed pretty suspect or something, because not one of them stopped for us. When they were close enough to get a good look at us they speeded up again, splashing great mountains of water all over us as often as not. We took to having a pile of gravel in our hands and chucking it at them as they sped away. At least it got rid of some of the anger.

So we trudged home in silence. Nine long wet miles, and barely a word spoken. Not by me, anyway. No way was I going to be friendly with Charlie Ferguson after what he'd put me through.

At one point, mind you, my anger got too much for me.

'So what about Gina?' I said, almost spitting the words out.

'What about her?' he answered, as though he hadn't the slightest idea what I was talking about.

'I thought you were going out with her.'

'Yeah. I am.'

'So why the Castletown hot dog?' I ventured.

'Huh?'

I explained.

'Why not?' he said, when he understood what I was on about. 'There's more than one fish in the sea. You take all you can get. Life's too short, Jesse. Life's too short to mess about with all that nice guy stuff!'

I spat on the ground, as close to his foot as I dared. I was disgusted with him. Disgusted with everything.

It was half-past one by the time we got back to Greywater. Half-past one in the morning. I was worried my mum would be sitting up waiting for me, but it turned out she'd gone to bed early, assuming I was still up at the Club. (I'd never got round to mentioning that we were off to Castletown.)

I stripped off my sodden clothes and had a boiling hot shower before collapsing into bed. And waking up with a stinking cold.

And as if that wasn't enough, the next time Responsible Bus Driver was on Youth Club duties, he didn't half give us a piece of his mind.

'That's the last time I take you boys anywhere!' he bawled. 'I've never been so ashamed in my whole life. I give up my time to take you on a trip, and look how you repay me! And I'm particularly disappointed in YOU, Jesse Flood,' he said, eyeballing me. 'I didn't think you were that sort at all!'

Sniggers from the back.

'I'm not, actually,' I wanted to say. But there was no point. Catch 22. Whatever you say you lose. And I'd never be trusted again.

It turned out, I heard on the grapevine, that two-timing Charlie had been trying all evening to get this Castletown girl to go walkies with him, but the only way she'd agree was if her friend Tracey could come too. And Tracey, for some reason I'll never understand, insisted he got ME to join them. Aaargh! What a nightmare!

It was made even worse a few weeks later, when me and my mum were shopping in the Co-op in Castletown. We got to the checkout and this female looks up from the till and gives me the filthiest grin you've ever seen.

'Hiya, Jesse,' she says. 'Wanna come into the storeroom with me?'

It was her! Tracey AppleGum! I couldn't get out of there quick enough.

'Someone you know?' said Mum, trying to keep up with me as I raced down the street.

No reply. What can you say?

I gave up on Youth Club soon after that. Gave up on the opposite sex, too. More trouble than they're worth.

Now That's What
I Call Living!

That's enough about me for a while. Here's a wee story.

This guy, let's call him Jimmy, he lives with his family in an old school bus in New Mexico. There's him, his mom and pop and his five brothers and sisters, all squeezed into this clapped-out old hippy bus. They're driving it all round New Mexico and up into California, stopping off in different places – just bumming about, basically.

Only one day the poor old bus gives up the ghost. 'Dag nabbit,' it wheezes, at the end of one too many hot and dusty days, 'I've had just about enough of getting my kicks on ol' Route 66, or wherever we are. I'm off to meet the great bus-builder in the sky.'

So when they get to the next bend Pop turns the wheel and the clapped-out hippy bus, for the first time in its life, refuses to cooperate. Yes, for the very first time in its long and obedient life, it grabs hold of the dying embers of the Swinging Sixties, embraces the spirit of flower power and revolution, and does what it damn well wants. Heads for eternity. Carries straight on and off the road, down the bank, and ends up upside-down on its roof.

And would you believe it, but Mom and Pop and Jimmy and the other five little Brokers all clamber out of the doors and windows, not a scratch on one of them.

And Pop says, once he's done a quick headcount, 'Right. That's the last time I live in a bus.' And off he goes and buys a tent. A big old ex-army tent.

And they're away on their travels again, pitching it here and there, and life's not so bad till one day the poor old tent gets sucked out of the ground by some sort of a tornado, up into the air and away. And there's Mom and Pop and Jimmy and the rest staring up at the sky, nothing between their puny bodies and God. And Pop says, 'Right, that's the last time I live in a tent.'

So they head for the coast, where he buys an old ramshackle boat. One that's seen better days, of course, or how would he have been able to afford it?

In they pile, Mom, Pop, Jimmy and the rest, though the poor unfortunate children have never set foot on the water before in their lives, not that you actually set foot on water but you know what I mean, and off they sail.

And they're planning to live off the creatures of the sea, only none of them has a single clue about fishing. Two fishes they catch that first day, two fishes between the seven of them, and good old J.C., our Lord and Saviour, might have been able to feed the five thousand in such a fashion, but Mom and Pop, no way.

A storm blows up and they can't get back into the harbour. So they're out all night, tossed and buffeted by the elements at their most extreme. And Pop's not all that knowledgeable about sailing a boat, I'm afraid, not having had much experience in matters maritime, since he was brought up just about as far from the sea as a body can get, but he manages. Just about, he manages.

And when they eventually get back to dry land, Mom and Jimmy and the five storm-tossed brothers and sisters all rise up and say, like they've been rehearsing it for days till they're word-perfect, though they haven't and actually it's just coincidence that they're all saying the same thing at the same time. 'Listen up, Pop,' they say. 'That's the last time we live in a boat. It's time to get your act together, start living in the real world, find yourself a proper job and us a proper home!'

And he does, sort of. He gets them a big trailer to live in and he turns himself into a taxi-driving part-time gardener (though he doesn't know a lot about gardening, and he thinks he can drive a cab the way he used to drive that poor old bus, which isn't well at all).

And Jimmy and the rest of the gang have a some-what more conventional childhood from then on, with a roof over their heads, and schools, and half-decent food and suchlike. But every single one of them has been touched by strangeness, affected by their unconventional upbringing in such a way that they can never quite fit into the narrow parameters of other people's expectations. In other words, they're weird. Sure certain weird.

One grows up to be an artist in Ulan Bator, another becomes a wrestler in Southern Winnipeg and a third ends up as a lion tamer in Outer Mongolia. (I'm exaggerating somewhat here, because I actually haven't a clue what they did – it didn't tell you in the *Sunday Information*, where I read about this Jimmy guy, but what the heck, I'm sure that's what story-telling's all about, making it up as you go along.) And each one of them goes their own crazy way.

And Jimmy? Well, I can tell you a bit more about Jimmy. Jimmy saves lives. Jimmy studies, and passes exams, and studies, and passes more exams, and Jimmy becomes a doctor.

And not for Jimmy the cosy but relatively unchallenging existence of a town medic in the American Midwest, oh no. Jimmy goes to the Congo. Jimmy goes to a village in the middle of Africa, a village of great poverty, a village with a load of disease and no medical facilities whatsoever. There Jimmy sets up a hospital, and there Jimmy saves lives. A whole shedful of lives.

Word spreads, and people come from miles around, on donkeys, on foot, carried in on makeshift stretchers. They camp out in the courtyard, hundreds of them, and they wait until Jimmy can heal them. Or as many of them as he can, anyway. As many as his meagre supply of medicines allows.

And the people come to love Jimmy, for he has a special gift of healing. He can heal with drugs and he can heal with his hands – he can cure the ill and somehow he finds he can even cure some of those poor unfortunates touched by witchcraft and sorcery. He's thin and he has pale skin and he wears little round wire-rimmed John Lennon glasses like his father before him. Well, all those Congolese think he's the strangest creature they've ever seen, but they respect him. They respect him and they love him.

For he can cure anything, just about. He can even cure AIDS, they say. He comes to your bed, when no one else will come to your bed, holds your hand, when no one else will hold your hand, and he talks to you gently, partly in your language and partly in his. And you don't understand what he's saying and you don't know how holding your hand is going to make you feel better, but it does.

Well, maybe it's the pills Jimmy gives you or the morphine he injects into your arm, but mainly it's the touch of his hand and the warmth of his smile and the way he makes you laugh even when you've no idea what it is he's trying to say. That's what helps the fear and the pain and the loneliness fade, and that's what helps you sleep.

But can he really cure AIDS, this weedy little, spec-cy little, white man? Well, maybe he doesn't actually cure it, but if there's enough medicine, and you keep taking the pills every day like he says, then it seems like you can stay alive. You can feel a lot better and the people let you back in among them again. And you can take care of your family for a while longer, and what greater gift is there than that?

And every now and again Jimmy ups and leaves. He ups and leaves his hospital in the care of the African doctors and nurses he's trained, and he flies back home to America and he begs for drugs and money to carry on with his work.

And he travels all around, giving talks to business-men and politicians and church groups and colleges and anyone who'll listen. And he tells them about women dying for the lack of clean water, and children dying for the want of a pill that costs fifty cents in the United States. And he shows them slides of hunger and slides of disease and he shows them pictures that would make anyone with even half a heart cry.

And this Jimmy, he shows all these people a photo of a girl who was brought in one night. She'd been carried twenty miles. She's completely bald and her body is wasted away, her arms and legs are like matchsticks. Then, would you believe it! Here's a picture of her a few months later, with a beautiful head of hair, chubby cheeks, and a smile that'd charm the birdies down from the trees!

So reach into your pockets, says Jimmy, deep deep down into the capacious folds of your Western wealth. Because the poor are suffering. All over the world the poor are suffering, and it's up to you to do what you can to help the poor and the lame and the blind and the ill and the wounded.

And they do! They open their wallets, the hard-nosed businessmen. They unlock their vaults, the tight-fisted bankers. They clear out their drug cupboards, the merciful medics, and they give our Jimmy what he needs to carry on for another few months.

And the drugs he gets, he uses to heal. And the money he gets, he spends on cleaning up the water system so there's no more typhoid. And the rest of the money he spends on schools. Schools to educate people. And one of the things he makes sure they teach people in the schools and the villages is how to avoid getting AIDS, because before Jimmy arrived no one was even talking about it. They were dropping like flies from this terrible disease but they had no idea what caused it, no idea how to prevent it, and they were so scared of it that they wouldn't even accept that there was such a thing. Even the government wouldn't accept that there was such a thing.

So that's our Jimmy. That's what he does, that boy I was telling you about, the one who grew up in a hippy bus, trudging up and down the highways and byways of New Mexico.

And it's all true, because I read it in a Sunday paper a while ago. I've changed the names and the facts a bit, like you do, but it's pretty well all true.

And if you're still wondering why I'm telling you Jimmy's story, not mine, then you haven't got the hang of what I'm on about at all. I'm on about life! I'm on about not just getting by, not just living your three-score-years-and-ten the same old way everyone else does. I'm on about getting on out there and doing something real.

Because that's what I call living, Jimmy Boy!

That's what I call living!

Sinister Goings-on

Jesse Flood – Age 8-9

Maybe it's because I'm left-handed. Maybe that's why I don't fit in.

I'm not supposed to be left-handed. It's all Ed Hawkins's fault. Ed was this boy who moved into the area when I was about eight. He'd come from England, so he spoke in a funny accent. He wore tidy, English sort of clothes, he spoke all posh, and he didn't live in town, he lived on a farm.

Before Ed Hawkins came to school I was right-handed. No doubt about it. I wrote with my right hand and I threw a ball with my right hand. I used scissors with my right hand and I did just about everything with my right hand.

And most of the time I did it well. I was top of the class in writing and top of the class in maths and Miss Wilde, who was our teacher in the Junior School, was delighted with me. Which was lucky, because she certainly lived up to her name – she could be an absolute dragon if she didn't like you.

But when Ed Hawkins came to school everything changed. Within a week HE was top of the class – top of the class in writing, top of the class in maths, top of the class in art (which was the one thing I'd never been much good at, to tell you the truth. If I try to draw a dog, it always ends up more like a worm). He could run a whole lot faster than me and he was MUCH better at football. I liked him, though. He wasn't the same as everyone else. He didn't mind being different, didn't mind being clever, and he had a wicked sense of humour. You should have heard him pretending to be Miss Wilde! When she was well out of the way, of course.

So I wasn't jealous or anything, even though Ed was teacher's favourite now, instead of me. No, I always hung out with him after school, while he wait-ed for his dad to get round to picking him up. Often he'd come over to my house and we'd kick a football up and down the garden till his dad came looking for him.

Sometimes I'd go back with Ed to his farm and we'd mess about in the barn, jumping off hay bales, playing at action movies, or if we were feeling a bit less energetic we'd sit in the studio and watch his dad painting. His dad was a famous artist, according to Ed, not that anybody round here had ever heard of him, so far as I know, and he did these massive great modern art things, all streaks and splashes and stains and stuff. It was great to watch.

Apart from the fact that he was my friend, there was something about Ed. Something that was like me, but not like me. Something that made me watch him, everything he did, even more closely than I watched his dad. I watched him in the classroom and I watched him in the playground. I watched him eating his dinner and I watched him feeding the chickens, and all the time I was trying to work out what it was that was so different about him. It wasn't just the way he talked or the way he dressed. It wasn't just the fact that he was English and he lived on a farm, and his dad was supposed to be a famous artist. No, it was something else.

And then the boy who sat next to me, Joey Fitz, had to leave school suddenly – I heard a while later that the police had caught him throwing lighted matches into post boxes, but I don't know if it's true or not. So, anyway, the space next to me was free and Miss Wilde asked would anyone like to sit there, and

Ed Hawkins put his hand up, and I was happy.

So Ed was in against the wall and I was sitting next to him, but right from the start there was something strange about it, something awkward. Somehow our arms kept bashing into each other. It never used to happen with Joey Fitz. I watched Ed doing his maths and I thought about why our pens kept clashing and our elbows kept bashing and then I worked it out. He was holding his pen in his left hand! He was left-handed!

I'd never really thought about anyone being left-handed before. It just wasn't something that I'd really been aware of. But suddenly it all made sense. Ed Hawkins was left-handed, and he was MUCH better at maths than me! In fact, he was much better than me at just about everything. So that was it, I decided. That was the trick.

So, I know it sounds silly, and I bet you don't believe me, but I swopped. There and then I swopped. I put my pencil in my left hand, I pressed the point on the paper, and I started writing.

At first it felt really awkward and my writing was hopeless, all scrawls and scribbles and you couldn't read a word of it. But it's amazing how much progress you can make if you're really determined. And determined I was, because I was totally convinced that this was the way to make everything right again. That this was the way to make myself just as good as Ed the wonderboy Hawkins.

So I scrawled and I scribbled and I practised late into the night and all weekend, drawing straight lines, drawing circles, writing my name, practising my signature, writing, writing, writing. And you know what they say. Practise makes perfect. Well, not quite perfect, but I was certainly getting the hang of it.

And Ed helped me with my maths, explaining the bits I couldn't understand, because he was that sort of a guy and soon I was getting everything just about right there, too. Mind you, he was a long way ahead of me at writing, now. Miss Wilde kept asking me why my work was so untidy all of a sudden. But she wasn't very observant, you know. I don't think she ever even noticed that I'd switched to my left hand, and I certainly never told her.

So, in time, my writing got better until it was just about as tidy as it had been when I was using my right. And now I'm left-handed! I can still write with the other one if I have to, like when I fell off my bike and had my left arm in plaster for six weeks, but it's not very tidy. In fact, it's nearly as bad as when I first started writing with my left. It's funny how you stop being able to do things once you stop doing them.

I'm not completely left-handed, mind you. Only for writing. I still throw a ball with my right hand and brush my teeth with my right hand, and play table tennis and hold my knife and use scissors, all with my right hand. It's only writing that I do with my left.

The trouble is, it's got me muddled. If someone asks me directions I'll say, 'You go down the road and you turn left, no right, and you come to the Post Office and you turn right, no left, no RIGHT and . . .' You see, I've got them all mixed up in my brain. I just can't tell the difference.

And it seems to affect the way I think, too. If there are two things to remember, I always muddle them up. I'm OK if there are three or four or even five, but if there are only two and they're a bit similar, like left and right, then I'm hopeless. Take my Aunty Claire, for example. She's got two little girls and they're not twins but they're nearly twins and one's called Sophie and one's called Theresa and I never never NEVER get it right. You'd think I'd get it right half the time, at least. But no. I just about never do. I'm trying too hard, I suppose.

So why am I telling you all this? Just because I think changing from right to left maybe affected my brain, somehow. Because before I was fine, and now I'm a mess. Before I was pretty much like everyone else, and now I'm not. Now I'm different. Now I'm off the rails, sort of. Now I'm SINISTER.

Because I looked it up, that word sinister, in the dictionary the other day. I wanted to put it in a story I was writing – I was just checking I'd got the spelling right, and I found out something spooky. Real spooky. It doesn't just mean evil and criminal and villainous and Stephen King and Alfred Hitchcock and wicked stepmothers and Cruella De Ville in *The Hundred and One Dalmatians* and Gollum in *The Lord of the Rings* and that nasty wizard guy in *Harry Potter*. No, it also means, would you believe it, LEFT-HANDED! It does. I promise you. Look it up if you don't believe me.

Mind you, maybe it wasn't all Ed Hawkins's fault, the way I turned out. Maybe it had something to do with what came later. Five years later.

The Big One

Jesse Flood – Age 14

I'm lying in bed, the pillow pulled tightly over my head, like I always do when they're rowing. Either that or I turn my music up loud. That or I walk.

I used to intervene. I used to stand between Mum and Dad and yell, 'Stop it! *Stop it!* STOP IT!'

But it never did any good. She'd raise her voice, to drown out my yelling. I'd raise my voice, to drown out hers. And Dad would just stand there, one eye on the television, waiting for it all to blow over. Pretending it was nothing whatsoever to do with him. Just another silly display of female histrionics on Mum's side, childish hysteria on mine. He'd say so, in that quiet, controlled, oh so maddening voice of his.

'Now calm down, Martha. There's no need to get so emotional.'

She'd freak out then, maybe even start swearing at him. I hate it when she swears. So I'd start swearing at both of them. And then they'd turn on me.

'Jesse, how dare you use language like that! Go to your room!'

Yeah, blame me. Blame me for the fact that you two can't get on. Blame me for the fact that you can't stand the sight of one another. Blame me for keeping you together all these years. And while you're at it, even if I wasn't born yet, you might as well blame me for bringing you together in the first place, when anyone with half a brain should have been able to see you were about as well matched as a kangaroo and a sausage. Go on, pin all the blame on me. Maybe that'll stop you blaming each other.

So I do what they say. I walk out on them. Walk out and leave them to it. Climb the stairs and let them get on with it. Because it never did do any good, trying to stop them.

This time they're at it, full volume, and it's the pillow. Pulled tight, over my ears. Pulled tight, to block out the anger. And then I hear my name. It's weird how one word can cut through the barrier of silence, how one little word can seem so much louder than any other.

'But what about Jesse?' I hear my Dad saying.

I put the pillow away and sit upright, ears on stalks.

'*Jesse!*' she yells. '*Suddenly you're so concerned about Jesse!*'

She's lost it. You can tell just in the way she says those few words that she's completely lost it.

'I've always been concerned about Jesse, Martha. You know that.' Slowly. Calmly. Making sure he doesn't slur.

'*Oh yeah? If you've been so concerned about Jesse all these years, how come you never managed to hold down a decent job for longer than six months? If you're so concerned about Jesse, how come there's never enough money to keep him in decent clothes because you drink it all? If you're so concerned about Jesse, how come you let him do whatever he likes, any hour of the day or night?*'

Silence. No answer.

'*And if you're so concerned about your beloved Jesse, how come it's always me that has to yell at him to get up in time to catch the train? How come it's always me that has to take time off work to go to those horrendous parent teacher meetings where they tell me what a lazy, good-for-nothing slob he's turning out to be. Just like his father before him, that's what I tell them. Yes, how come all you do for your precious Jesse is sit on your backside watching daytime tele-*

vision and waiting for the pub to open? Tell me this, just tell me this, Samuel Flood, if you're so concerned about your darling Jesse, why do you never EVER choose to spend any time with him?'

'Look, Martha. I'm doing my best. You know I've a problem with my nerves.'

'A problem? I'm the one with a problem! And it's YOU – Samuel James Flood, YOU – the original number one WASTE OF SPACE! Why, oh why, didn't I listen to my poor mother the night before our wedding? "If you want to pull out, Martha," she said, "I'll be right behind you." Well it was a bit late for pulling out, then, wasn't it?'

I think I know what she means. I'd seen the wedding photos.

'Martha, please.' Fierce whisper. 'Keep your voice down.'

'Why? Why in the name of God should I? In case your precious Jesse hears the facts of life? He knows all that, for goodness sake, no thanks to you. And it's about time he knew the real facts. The facts of my life. Fact one: This marriage is a complete sham. It always has been and it always will be. Fact two: You're a no-good beer-swilling pig, Samuel Flood. You always were, and I only married you because you went and got me pregnant. Fact three: I've

89

given you fourteen of the best years of my life and what have I got in return? Sweet F.A. Fact four: I am leaving you, Samuel. I have had more than enough of you and your nerves, you and your petty inadequacies, you and your lies, you and your damn promises. I have given you so many chances to get your act together, Samuel Flood, and you have failed. Completely and utterly failed.'

Silence.

'I have tried and I have tried and I have TRIED to make this a good marriage. I have tried and I have tried and I have TRIED to love you, Samuel Flood, but I have finally realized that I never did, not really, and I never will. I simply cannot love someone who loves the bottle more than me. You have had every chance to prove to me that that is not the case, and failed every time. So this is it, Samuel. I mean it. I promised myself that the next time you came home stinking of beer I would leave you, and I am. Here is my suitcase, all packed. I am going to pick up that case, walk out the front door, take your precious new Ford and disappear from your life for ever. And I warn you, Samuel Flood, don't try and stop me.'

'But what about Jesse, Martha? You can't just—'

'Oh, do shut up about Jesse, you stupid man! This is not about Jesse, it's about you and me. And it's about time I

gave some thought to my own needs, Samuel, because you sure as hell never will. You've always put yourself first, so now it's my turn. You can look after Jesse, for now. I've done my best with him, under the circumstances. It's about time you shouldered some of the parental responsibility.'

So this is it. The big one. They've been leading up to it for years, of course, but I never thought it'd actually happen. I never thought either of them would be strong enough to face up to life on their own.

And now it's happening. Mum's leaving. She doesn't even come up to say goodbye. I twitch the curtain and watch her march down the drive without even a backward look, fling her suitcase into the boot, climb into the driving seat, rev up the engine, crash the gears and go.

Bye, Mum. I'll see you around, maybe.

I find the letter in my schoolbag the next morning. I'm on the way to school but I'm not on the way to school, if you know what I mean.

It's tucked in next to my books. I pull it out and recognize the writing. I read it, with tears pouring down my face. I don't give a damn who sees me.

I'm sorry, Jesse. I'm really sorry to be doing this. None of it's your fault. You must know that.

I love you, my sweet boy. I love you so much, but I just can't live with your father any more. I know he'll never leave me, so I've no choice but to leave him, before he drags me down with him.

I'm really sorry I couldn't tell you I was going. I'm really sorry I didn't say goodbye. But I was scared. Scared I'd break down and cry. Scared you'd talk me out of leaving, or I'd talk myself out of it.

This is the hardest thing I've ever done, Jesse, but I'm sure it's right. I'm sure that in the long run it'll be better for all of us.

I can't tell you where I'm going yet, love, and I don't want you to try and find me. I need space. I need time to get my head together.

I thought of asking you to come with me, but it wouldn't be fair. It wouldn't be right to take you away from your friends, from your school, from all the things that are good in your life.

And I'm not leaving your father for anyone else, in case that's what you think. It's not about that. It's never been about that.

I'll be in touch, Jesse. I don't want anything more

to do with him, I'm afraid, because being together is no good for either of us. But I have no intention of losing you, my darling boy, so as soon as I possibly can, I'll be in touch. I'll send a message through Beth, and you can come and stay.

I know all this will be really horrible for you, Jesse. I know things haven't been easy for some time, and that this is the last thing you need right now.

I'm really, really sorry for all the pain we've both caused you, my lovely boy. I'm really, really sorry I haven't been a good enough mother.

I pray that one day you'll find it in your heart to forgive me.

xxx Mum

I'm thinking back. Back to the days of the Green Lady. Back to the days when there was someone to watch over me, someone to make things right. When I could come in from school and she'd be there, reading in her big squashy chair, or out in the garden with her plants.

In truth, there weren't many of those sort of days, because Mum was nearly always out at work when I came home. Well, somebody had to bring in the money.

But I remember one particular day she was there, and I was glad of it. Very glad.

Jesse Flood – Age 10

It was the year after I'd gone all sinister, all left-handed. I'd taken my bike up to the top of the hill above the house, right to the very top, and the plan was to zoom down it at full speed. The brakes weren't up to much on that old bike – I'd been asking Dad to tighten them for ages, but he never got around to it. Never really got around to anything much.

Still, there was never any traffic on the Shore Road, the road that ran along the bottom, so I thought I probably wouldn't need to stop. Not completely, anyway.

So, like I said, the idea was to keep going, all the way down the hill, then turn sharp right and carry on as far as you could along the flat without pedalling. Staying on as long as possible, down the road, all through the final wobbles like a slow bicycle race till you ground to a halt and had to put a foot down to prevent yourself crashing to the ground.

There was a stick in the grass to mark where I'd got to last time, way past everyone else, but I was still determined to beat it, to set a new Jesse Flood Freewheeling World Record.

So off I go, down the hill, standing in the saddle and pushing down hard hard hard hard at the start to get up enough speed – you're only allowed four pushes, that's the rule, and then you have to just let the wind carry you. But it's steep, that hill. Very steep. So I'm going faster, faster, picking up speed till the air's rushing through my face and I'm flying.

Coming up closer to the junction, all I can see ahead of me is Mrs Brennan's house, on the other side of the road. There's supposed to be someone standing at the bottom to warn you if there's any traffic coming, to warn you if you need to stop or if you can carry on, round the corner on to the Shore Road. That's the way everyone else does it – gets one of their mates to signal if it's OK. But I can't be bothered with that. It takes half the excitement out of it, and I haven't got anyone I want to ask, anyway.

So I touch the brakes only slightly, ever so slightly, to slow me down just enough to get round the bend without hitting the kerb on the other side. You don't want to brake too much, of course, or you'll be going too slow on the flat and you won't get anywhere near the World Record.

But I've got it all wrong this time. I must have pushed down harder than usual on the pedals, because I'm shooting down the hill, close to the bend, and I can tell there's something badly wrong. And it's not that there's any traffic coming, because my ears are out on stalks and I'm sure I'd be able to tell. No, the coast's clear, the road's empty, but it's something else.

I'm going too fast! Too fast to go round!

I slam on my brakes at the last minute, knowing there's no way I'm going to make it. But it's too late, and they're worse than useless, anyway, like I said. It's not so much a slamming on of brakes, more like a gentle caress of rubber on rim.

So I'm leaning over, desperately hoping I'll be able to guide the bike round by the power of positive thought but knowing for sure that I won't, and then a sickening CRASH! My wheel thumps into the kerb on the opposite side of the road and I'm flying up and over the handlebars, straight into Mrs Brennan's hedge.

And it wouldn't be so bad if I'd stayed in the hedge, or gone through it on to her lawn, but no such luck. It's one of those springy sort of hedges, and I bounce back out and hit the pavement, hard. And hear a crack.

A crack and a searing pain, running up my left arm. A crack, and I'm groaning. A crack, and there's Mrs Brennan, coming running out of her house.

'Oh, dear! Oh, you poor boy! What happened?'

She fusses over me for a while, flapping her arms up and down like she's about to take off, and then she pulls herself together, helps me up on to my feet and into her living room, and lays me down on the sofa. My arm's killing me, and my legs aren't much better. She's full of fuss, full of questions, and I don't answer one of them.

She goes out into her hallway, then, and I can hear her ringing Mum. She knows who I am, knows who my mum is, because they go to church together. Everyone knows who everyone else is, in a small town like this, it's just that half of them never talk to the other half.

And while she's ringing, a cat comes into the room and starts snuffling round me. It climbs up on to the sofa, trying to be nice, but the pain makes me angry. I push it off, on to the floor, and my arm hurts even more.

I lie there for a while, with my eyes tight shut to try and keep the feeling down, to try and block out Mrs Brennan's fussing, and suddenly there's Mum, puffing and panting. She's come running down the hill – running, because we haven't got a car any more. Dad's been banned from driving, see, and we couldn't afford to keep it. Mum's been working up in town three days a week, so she's been able to use the train to get to work. Only this is one of her days off, thank God.

'Oh Jesse! My poor Jesse!' she cries, and she drops down on her knees and puts her arms around me. She holds me tight and I feel the tears forming in my eyes, the tears I've been fighting.

I drink the hot sugary tea I've been given, even though it's cold now. And then Mum helps me up and across the room and out on to the drive where Mrs Brennan's got her little car waiting.

Mum sits next to me in the back with her arm around me, and the pain's something awful, especially every time we go over a bump. I've never noticed it before, even when I had to walk home that night with Charlie Ferguson, but the road to Castletown is terrible for bumps, especially with old Mrs Brennan driving.

So off we go to the hospital, up in Castletown, because like I told you, this town's got nothing. And she's lovely, my mum. She's so soft and warm and she can make me smile with all the silly things she says, even when the pain's nearly too much to bear. She's fussing, but it's mother fussing, not stranger fussing, and it's good. And we're close. And everything's all right.

She could do that, see. She could make things better. No matter what happened, she could make things better. I wish she was here right now, my mum. I wish she was still around. But she's the last Green Lady up on One Tree Hill. The last Green Lady and we've chopped her out of our lives.

part two

Flynn

Jesse Flood – Age 14¼

I don't want you to think I haven't any friends. I have. Dominic Flynn. Known as Flynn.

(Ed went back to England after a couple of years, by the way. His dad never really took to the North. No one here had much interest in all that modern art stuff. They thought the man was a complete wally and took the piss out of him every chance they got.)

Flynn lives up near the lighthouse, with his sick mother. He's got three older brothers – one's an engineer, one's a teacher and the third's a dentist. The one who's an engineer lives in Australia, the one who's a teacher lives in Scotland, and the one who's a dentist lives in Belfast.

So he's got these well-off, clever, high-achieving brothers. But Flynn's a bit like me, only more so. He doesn't give a damn what anyone thinks.

Mind you, in many ways he's quite a bit different

103

from me. For one thing, he's twenty-three. Flynn used to have an old Second World War air-raid shelter in his garden. One of the last around. Bit of an historical heirloom, by all accounts. Only it doesn't exist any more. Flynn took it upon himself to blow it up, for some strange reason. He wanted to see if it was bomb-proof. Hell of a mess. That's the sort of crazy guy he is.

Flynn says Youth Club's really naff. Says he'd never set foot in one. So these days, long hot summer days, whenever my dad thinks I'm up playing table tennis, I'm not. I'm over at Flynn's, he's smoking his stock of ready-rolled roll-ups (I can't stand the smell of them, me, but I'd never tell Flynn that), we're both tucking into his mum's whiskey and listening to his dad's old Beatles records.

Flynn thinks *She Came in Through the Bathroom Window* is the best song ever written, and I must say I'm inclined to agree with him. Through a haze of cigarette smoke and whiskey fumes, anyway.

He's not dumb, though, Flynn, even if he has got a strange taste in music and looks a bit like a snake – long and thin and pitted. He's got a killer wit, and he's planning to become a novelist when he gets his act together, so he says – that or a dentist like his brother and his dad.

His dad's dead, though – died when Flynn was sixteen. He was the only dentist in Greywater and people still remember his fondness for whipping out your teeth as soon as you opened your mouth. No preventitive dentistry for him. No scrapes and polishes and quiet little lectures on the benefits of regular brushing, regular flossing, a shiny new apple a day. Oh no, open it wide, open it wide, open it wider and tug! So they tell me.

Famous, too, Flynn senior, for the fact that he always seemed to go a bit easy on the anaesthetic. A little pain never hurt anyone, was his motto. It's the price you pay for neglect. By the time he died, and he kept on working right up to the end, just about anyone with any teeth left had switched to the new young dentist in Castletown. You could hardly blame them. In fact, Greywater must have the lowest average tooth count of any town in the developed world. A mouthful of gaps. Gaps and falsies. It's no wonder people don't smile much round here. Well, not when I'm about, anyway.

And Flynn's mum, well she spends most of the day

in bed. She's been ill for years, and Flynn has to stay and look after her. That's why he never went to college. That's why he never left Greywater. The older brothers all ended up with degrees, jobs, wives, children. But Flynn, because he was the last, got stuck in this boring little dead-end town. And you know what happens if you stay in a boring little dead-end town all your life? You turn out boring, too. Either that or you go mad. Flynn's ever so slightly mad, I'd say.

I'm heading that way too, probably. Well I'd rather be mad than boring, wouldn't you?

Anyway, the other night we were having this marathon Beatles session, me and Flynn. We listened to *Abbey Road* and *Sergeant Pepper's*. We even managed most of the *White Album*, and that takes some doing, especially on scratchy old vinyl. By the time I remembered where I was, it was way past my sleepy-time, and I'd had far too much whiskey. I only sip at it really, just to keep Flynn company. But five hours of sipping can make quite a hole in a bottle of Jameson's, never mind the effect it has on the brain of a fourteen-year-old, even if he is going on ninety-seven. So I staggered home, let myself in and there was Dad, waiting for me.

'And where do you think you've been?' he said.

I could hear the anger, or was it possibly concern, in his voice, even through the haze of my drunkenness.

'Youth Club,' I slurred.

'YOUTH CLUB!' he barked. 'Till half-past one in the morning!'

I tried to focus on the kitchen clock. It couldn't possibly be that late, could it? And anyway, what was Dad doing up at this time of night? He'd usually gone to bed in his own beer-filled stupor hours before.

My head was spinning so I plonked myself down on one of the wooden chairs, and next thing my stomach heaved and I found myself spewing, all over the floor.

'My God, son,' said Dad, recoiling as the mashed up, foul-smelling remains of carrots and whiskey trickled down his trouser leg on to the floor. 'What's happening here?'

I think that must have been the moment when he decided that things were out of control. That if he didn't take me in hand I was going to turn out just like him.

He brought me a mop and bucket and made me

clean up the mess I'd made. And then he helped me up to my room. He was gentle though. Not angry, like you'd think he'd be. He helped me into bed and put a basin on the floor beside me in case I needed it later. Didn't even go on about the state of my room.

He even looked in at me every now and again during the night. To check I hadn't choked on my own vomit, I suppose. I know, because he kept waking me, shaking my shoulders and saying, 'Are you all right, Jesse? Are you sure you're all right?'

I'd groan, turn over and go back to sleep. Leave me alone, Dad. Just leave me alone to get over it.

The next morning I woke with this blinding headache, and the sound of the hoover blasting away downstairs. I didn't even know we had a hoover, not since Mum left. I think I must have been under the impression she'd taken it with her in the Ford, or something.

And later on, after four cups of black coffee, Dad and I had a serious head-to-head.

'Where were you last night, Jesse? I need to know.'

I told him I'd been at Flynn's.

'I don't want you to go there again. He's a bad influence, and he's much too old for you.'

I couldn't accept that. I wouldn't.

'He's about my only friend, Dad. I can't just stop seeing him. And you're wrong about him, anyway. He's OK.'

In the end we agreed on a compromise. I could go up to Flynn's on Youth Club nights, but I had to promise to be home by midnight.

'And NO MORE BOOZE!'

I was happy to agree. I never wanted to touch alcohol again.

'And do you want me to hoover your room, now I've found out where the damn thing lives?'

'No, it's all right, Dad. Leave it here. I'll do it.'

Charlie Ferguson

So is Dad right? Is Flynn a bad influence? Is he leading me astray, leading me off into all sorts of ways of thinking, ways of being that I wouldn't have, shouldn't have, found otherwise? Or is he just giving me a bit of breathing space, a place where I can take things easy and not feel judged, not feel criticized. A place where I can try out different ways of thinking, different ways of being without the cold hand of Greywater convention hovering inches above my head.

I'd have said the latter. I'd have defended Flynn against anyone, stuck up for his right to be himself and my right to spend as much time with him as I want.

But one night things change. One night I go over to his place and find him in a terrible state. Slumped in a kitchen chair, his head in his hands.

'What's wrong, Flynn?' I ask, searching for clues in

the back of his head, in the state of the room. 'Is it your mum? Is she bad?'

He shakes his head. No.

'What is it then?'

I've never seen him like this before. He's always in control, in that laid-back Flynn sort of way. I don't like him like this. I don't know where I stand. Don't know what to make of it.

He doesn't move. Doesn't talk. It takes me ages to get any more out of him. Ages of prompting, of silence, of walking round the room picking up things and putting them back down again, of pretending to go out and leaving him to it.

'It's Charlie,' he says, eventually, lifting his head up and looking at me through his long dark hair, through his deep, brown, sorrowful eyes. 'Charlie Ferguson.' And then he goes quiet again.

Quiet for so long that I've enough time to run through in my mind the whole short history of me and Charlie Ferguson.

I haven't seen him around much lately. He stopped going to Youth Club a little while after I did, so I heard. But for rather different reasons.

At first he was OK, Charlie. He appeared out of nowhere, from Scotland, determined to make his mark. And right from the start I could see he was the sort of person who demanded attention. Who wasn't just happy to fade into the background. Who says, here I am, this is me, what are you going to do about it?

We were too different to ever get close, but I'd nothing against him, not at first, anyway. A bit loud, a bit full of himself, but OK. At least he was an individual, not a sheep. A blast of fresh air, in a funny sort of way, in a town that desperately needed it.

But I'm good at keeping in the background. Good at watching people, working out what's going on, and it didn't take me long to see what was really happening on the Charlie Ferguson front. How things were changing.

Once he'd got himself established, got himself a circle of hangers-on, once he'd got some power, basically, I began to see the other side of him coming through. The cruel streak starting to show.

He'd come up to Youth Club, and he'd be friendly with almost everyone – the lads, the girls, even the Responsible Adults. But there was something else going on, something that it took me a while to spot.

Something he was very good at hiding. He was a bully, that's what it was. And a particularly nasty sort of bully, too.

What he was doing, and it took me a good while to actually catch him at it, was picking on the young ones behind people's backs. Getting them on their own. Threatening them. Making them hand over their money, their CDs, anything they had that he wanted. Giving one or two of them, the ones that tried to stand up to him, a bit of a going over.

And then, once he'd got them frightened enough, he started forcing some of the weaker ones to do his dirty work for him. Protection money, basically. Hand it over or else. That way Charlie could keep his hands clean and watch the goodies roll in.

Yeah, I know I've been hard on them myself sometimes, those kids, thrashing them at table tennis and such, but I mean, it's only a game. No one gets hurt. This was different.

Gina saw sense after a while, saw what Charlie was like deep down, and dumped him. I don't know what he did to her (or maybe it was her kid brother he did something to) or whether she found out he'd been two-timing her or whatever. But one night they were all over each other, like they'd been for ages, and the next it was like they'd never even met.

And I don't know what Gina said to her friends but soon none of the girls were even so much as talking to him. From ladies man to no-ladies man in one easy step. Maybe someone could teach me, only the other way round.

Anyway, things went from bad to worse in double quick time for Charlie, because next thing he was banned. Banned from Youth Club altogether. It was a big deal at the time, everyone was talking about it, because it had never happened before. Somehow the Responsible Adults found out what he was up to – the bullying and stealing and all, and hauled him and his father in for a special meeting.

He kept a low profile round Greywater after that, did Charlie. He was sporting one hell of a black eye the next time I saw him. From his dad, I suppose. A bit of a hard man, by all accounts.

And then I heard Charlie was hanging out with the druggies up in town. I wouldn't wish that on my worst enemy. They're bad news, that lot. So Flynn says, anyway.

*   *   *

Flynn. Slumped in his chair, with a lost look in his eyes. Me, struggling to understand, struggling to know how to respond. Endless cigarettes, till the room's so full of smoke I can hardly even see him. Eventually, painfully slowly, it worms its way out.

'I sold Charlie some stuff,' he says.

'Stuff?' I say. 'What sort of stuff?'

'You know,' he says, waving his roll-up at me as though it's a dumb sort of question. 'Stuff.'

And suddenly it clicks. Suddenly, I realize where Flynn's been getting his money from all this time. Realize what he's been up to whenever I've seen him in town, down on the prom, times he's been hanging out with people I don't even know, times he refuses to meet my eyes.

At last, I realize what the ready-rolled roll-ups are. Sometimes you're so naïve, Jesse Flood. Such an innocent.

Flynn tells me he's never had any trouble before. The quantity he's been selling, and the type of stuff it is wasn't likely to cause any problems. But this time he's worried. He could tell Charlie was already in a bad way when he saw him. It was obvious, just to look at him, that there was something seriously wrong. Something getting him down, way down. Flynn knew it, but it was his policy never to ask questions. Do the deal and get it over with.

A bit of grass, Charlie's usual. A few tabs, on the spur of the moment, from Flynn's personal supply, as a freebie for a good customer. To give Charlie a bit of a high, to let him fly. The poor kid looked like he needed it.

A Government health warning, laughingly delivered, and that's it. Off and enjoy yourself, son. Go forth and butterfly.

And Charlie's gone forth, all right. Forth, fifth, right out of sight. Missing, he is. Missing, in action. Missing and the police are out looking for him.

'I'm sure it's nothing,' I say, trying to calm Flynn down. 'I'm sure it'll be OK.'

Though I'm not sure. Not sure at all. And I'm not sure why I'm trying to be nice to Flynn, either. Because I'm furious at him. Furious at his stupidity. At how he's deceived me.

'Charlie'll be up in town with his mates,' I say. 'Or he'll have had another bust-up with his dad and gone to cool off somewhere.'

But he hasn't. I can tell he hasn't. I can feel it in my bones, that dull ache like the feeling I always get before something really nasty happens.

Search Party

They spend all day searching. All the next day, too. And a black cloud of depression settles over Flynn. Settles over Greywater, too.

The police call in volunteers, and a whole squad of them joins the search party. Anyone with time to spare and a reasonable knowledge of the area.

Dad offers to join them, and they take him on. It's the last thing I expect. He's always run a mile from any form of community service. But this is different, I suppose. This isn't just a way to make friends and influence people. This is the real thing.

I can see them. Everywhere I go, I can see them. Scouring the beach, the cliffs, the railway line, out to the Island, up by the reservoir. Everywhere.

And I'm doing it, too. Can't seem to stop myself, even though people keep coming up to me and saying, 'Go home, Jesse. There's enough of us.' That sort of thing.

And I know they really mean, 'He's here. He's here somewhere, and we don't want a kid to be the one to find him.'

And there's another reason I shouldn't be here, among them. Because I don't want to attract attention, I don't want them to start wondering why I'm so concerned, when I was never that bothered about Charlie before. I don't want anyone to start asking questions, especially the police. Don't want them to start putting two and two together, to start thinking maybe I know more than I'm letting on.

So I try and keep out of their way, though it's not easy, because there are so many of them. The whole town's crawling, like ants. All my secret places, places you never see another person from one month to the next.

And still I'm walking, walking, poking about in the long grass, looking behind rocks, peering down into the water, the old river bed, the reservoir. Pretending to myself that it's just walking. Just walking for the sake of it, like it's always been.

But it's different now. I can't enjoy it. I can't use it, one foot in front of the other, as a way of relaxing, as a way of resting my weary brain. And how could I possibly enjoy it, anyway, when I know exactly what it is I'm looking for, and I know what it's going to do to me when I find it.

I don't know how they know he hasn't just left town. That's what most people do round here. Just up and leave. Head for London, where the streets are paved with the homeless. They're gone for a few weeks and then they're back, most of them, back with their tails between their legs. Thinner, more broken, and with a sadness in their eyes. That's another story.

But somehow everyone knows Charlie hasn't left. They know he's around. That it's just a matter of time before they find him.

It's the waiting that's so hard to bear. The whole town either searching, or waiting. People on street corners, talking in whispers, shaking their heads. Looking up every time a helicopter flies over. Watching, as though the chopper's going to spell out the answers to everyone's questions.

And then they find him. Washed up off the Island. His body all bashed and beaten by the waves and the rocks, like some poor drowned sheep.

Word of mouth. Street corner whispers.

Confirmed by my dad. Confirmed by the television news.

Not that I see him, of course.

Not that my dad tells me whether he was the one who found him.

Not that I'd ever ask.

But there are things you don't need to see. Things that reappear in your mind, in your dreams, without you ever actually seeing them in the first place. Things that linger, things that haunt you.

I can't talk to Dad about it. It's so hard to talk to him about anything proper. Football, the weather, things like that he's fine. But anything real, like the state of the world, girls, Mum leaving, getting kicked out of school, no way.

It was Flynn who helped me out with that last one. Flynn who told me they'd no right to stop me going in and taking the exams. So I did. And he was right. No one said a word. And now I'm waiting for the results. Waiting to see if school will have me back after the holidays, or if I have to find somewhere else. Or maybe I'll just lie low, and stop going to school altogether. Pretend I'm sixteen. Get a job. Or run away to London.

I thought it was horrible, all that school business. I thought it was the end of the world when Mum left. But Charlie going missing. It sure puts things into perspective, doesn't it?

So I want to, I really want to talk to Dad about this Charlie thing. I want to, but I can't. I mean, what would I say?

I want to for my sake, because I need, I NEED to talk to someone about what I feel, what I know, someone other than Flynn.

God, I wish Mum was around. But then, I don't even know if I'd be able to talk to her. I don't know what I'd tell her and what I wouldn't tell her and what she'd do about it and whether it'd be fair on Flynn.

I want to talk about Charlie for Dad's sake, too. Because he looks terrible. It's really taken it out of him, being in the search party. Hoping you'll find something. Desperately hoping you won't. Knowing it's really important you do a thorough search. Knowing your heart will sink like a stone if you actually find what you're looking for.

But it's hard for me, too, being there just for Flynn. There, every time he rings. There, every time he calls round. When, deep down, I'm bloody angry at him.

Angry at the way he never told me what was going on, angry at the way he's been using me all this time, angry at the way he's using me now. I mean he's twenty-three, for God's sake. He's supposed to be grown-up. So why does he have to come and cry on my shoulder? Why does he have to draw me deeper and deeper into his nasty little web of lies?

Why does he always hang round with me, anyway? I'm nearly ten years younger than him. What is he, perverted or what?

Yeah, it's hard enough being there for Flynn. I can't support Dad, too.

And despite all the talk, all the gossip, nobody ever really knows what happened. We never find out if Charlie jumped or if he fell. We never know, any of us, whether everything just got too much for him – because who knows what goes on in someone else's life, in someone else's mind? – and he decided to end it all, loading up on the stuff he'd got off Flynn, stuff to take the pain away before he jumped.

Or whether he just took whatever he could lay his hands on, Flynn's and anything else going, purely for the sake of the high it'd give him. Purely for kicks.

Purely for a break from all the hassle, all the pressure. And then fell into the sea, by accident, in a drugged-out haze.

There's no word of a suicide note. No word of anyone talking to him on that final, fatal day. Which doesn't mean no one saw him. Doesn't mean no one was with him. It just means the police couldn't get anyone to talk. Which doesn't surprise me one bit.

The funeral's dreadful. Really dreadful. I'd never seen so many distraught people in one place. Everyone feels awful. Awful, if they liked Charlie. Even worse, if they didn't.

He was only a kid, only my age. He acted older, acted hard, swaggering round town like a nightclub bouncer. Swaggering round like he owned the place, even though he'd only been here a few months. But you could see through the mask. You could see the hurt little kid lurking underneath. I could anyway.

'Life's too short, Jesse.' That's what he'd said to me, that night, trudging home in the rain. 'Life's too short . . .'

How right he was. And how sad that is. Because what he meant was the complete opposite of this.

What he meant was take life in both hands and grab it, shake it, get everything you can out of it.

Don't throw it away. Don't just throw it away.

I'm sorry, Charlie. I'm sorry I wasn't able to be your friend. I'm sorry we were just too different. We both stood on the outside, looking in, but we'd never enough in common to come together. So I wasn't there for you when you needed a friend. I couldn't help you when you needed it the most.

I'm angry, Charlie. Not at you, but for you. You were never my favourite person – you knew that, I knew that. It couldn't be helped. It's just the way it was. But I'm really angry. Really angry at what life threw at you. Because it wasn't time for you to go. Whoever you were, whatever you'd done, you didn't deserve that.

You hadn't even become a proper person yet. You'd hardly even done any living. How is that fair?

Flynn doesn't show. I keep thinking I'll see him, lurking in the shadows at the back of the church, watching from behind a gravestone. I keep scanning the faces, trying to pick him out. But he isn't there.

He couldn't bear it, he told me later. Couldn't bear

the pain of it.

He threw away the tabs, though. Everything but the essentials. Flushed them down the toilet, he said. No more dealing. Personal consumption only.

We'll see.

Bellyflop

August. August and it's boiling. There's nothing
for it but to go down to the swimming pool,
down by the sea. It's not somewhere I go, generally.
Why's that?

It's the in thing to do. I'm not into doing the in
thing.

There are no cubicles in the changing room. You
have to strip off in front of everyone. Kids, staring at
your bits. Or giggling. Or both.

You get verrucas. Nasty little black holes in your
foot. They're a pain, and they take ages to get rid of. I
got them last time, even though I made sure I walked
in the disinfectant pool. Trouble is, loads of people
don't. You see them jumping across it. Risking breaking their legs, slipping on the wet tiles on the other
side, but jumping across it, anyway. Scared to get
their feet wet, no doubt. Scared to get their feet wet,
when they're about to go swimming! How thick can

you get? Mind you, half the time it's empty, anyway. All splashed out and no one's got round to refilling it. I don't think verruca prevention is top priority for the silly burghers of Greywater. Maybe I'll give that Jimmy Broker a call. He'd sort it out, no messing.

There are girls there. Looking at you. Watching you. Not in the changing room, stupid. No, lounging on their towels by the edge of the pool, lying on their side watching you through their dark glasses, their mirrored lenses. Rubbing suntan lotion into their glistening skin. Soaking up the rays of the sun and whispering to each other, things about you behind your back. (It's an outdoor pool, by the way, just in case you're wondering.)

Yeah, girls. Girls with hardly any clothes on. I want to look at them and I don't want to look at them. It's difficult.

I'm skinny, in swimming trunks. Skinny anyway, but you notice it more when I'm in trunks. All bones, I am. Skinny, pale and unattractive.

I never learnt to swim properly. Dad could never be bothered to teach me. Even when I was a kid, water was never good enough – he always preferred stronger forms of liquid. And school seemed to assume that because we lived by the sea we all knew how to swim, instinctively, like we were a race of mermaids or seals or something, so they didn't bother teaching us either. I had to find out by trial and error. Mostly error. Ends up, I look like a demented duck in the water. Splashing around, uncoordinated, just about managing to stay afloat. Drawing the attention of the bikini-clad sunworshippers in the worst possible sort of way.

I can't dive, and that's what you do here. That's what you come here for, if it's not just to get a tan. You climb to the top, slowly, slowly, till you're sure everyone's watching. You walk to the end of the board, preening yourself while you wait for the audience to settle down, and then you fly. I've always wanted to dive. Always wanted to be sleek and graceful and confident and accomplished, in at least one area of my life. Other than ping-pong. Well, you can't really be sleek and graceful at ping-pong, now can you?

So, there are a million and one reasons not to go down to the pool, a million and one reasons not to put myself forward for further ridicule. But it's boiling. The sweat's pouring off me. I rummage about under my bed, find my unfashionable trunks, cycle down the hill, chain up my unfashionable bike and go in. Into the changing room. Ignore the giggles.

Into the pool, into the water, splash about like a demented duck for about fifteen minutes till I get to the deep end, and then surface. I look around, blinking the water out of my eyes, and I see Yellow Lily, the one with the long blonde hair. Beautiful Yellow Lily, the girl of my dreams. Delicious Yellow Lily, my folk tale come true.

She's climbing the steps, the glistening water dripping off her delectable skin. She doesn't stop to be admired. Doesn't need to be admired. No, she just takes off. Out into the clear blue air. Streamlined, straight as an arrow, breaking the water with barely a splash. If anyone's a mermaid, it's Sophie Cameron, my Yellow Lily. If anyone's a creature from another world, it's her.

I swim another length, even more demented-duck like. Then I clamber out, climb the steps and prepare to dive. Crazy, I know, but I do it anyway. I look around, hoping no one's watching, and I catch Sophie's eyes. She's stretched out by the side of the pool now, the only one without sunglasses on, looking up at me.

Oh God, I know I'm going to make a fool of myself. Why do I do these things? What is it that drives me to put myself in such a position of ridicule? I pray, I jump, I pray, I fly. Fly through the air and I bellyflop. Crash, splash, aaah! Why do I always bellyflop?

The sting as my stomach whacks into the water, flat and hard. The tidal wave of a splash, that I know straightaway will have soaked everyone, inside the pool and out. All the girls, lying on their towels. Sophie Cameron, Yellow Lily, everyone.

I push the water from my eyes, look around, and I'm right. Some of them are angry. Others are laughing. But everyone's watching me. Every single person in the place is watching to see what I'll do next.

My chest's going red. Red to match my face. My chest's getting sore, sore as hell. But never say die, Jesse Flood. The only way to conquer your fear is to climb back up on that there horse and try again. To get back up those steps, back on those stilts, back on that bike, back on those two skinny legs and try again. And bellyflop. Again. What a surprise!

Don't look around this time. Don't look at Yellow

Lily. Stay under the water till the redness goes.

Swim like an otter, swim like a seal, glide through the water like a dolphin, a merman. As if.

I climb out. I don't catch her eye. I don't let her see me. My chest's still red. Red and sore. Red and stinging. Red and skinny and hairless and stupid. A demented duck, that's all I am. Jesse Flood, demented duck. Always so spectacularly unsuccessful at the things everyone else finds so easy.

Can't swim, can't dive, can't sail (I get seasick in the bath). Can't draw, can't tell left from right, can't play happy families, can't talk to girls. But whoopee, I'm a demon at ping-pong.

Into the changing room. Don't bother showering. Rub down your skin till it hurts. It hurts, and it deserves to hurt. Rub down your skin and you're dry. Throw on your clothes and cover your blushes. Throw on your clothes and go home.

And by the time I've cycled back up the hill I'm all sweaty again.

Small Town Saturday Boredom

Small town blues. Small town Saturday blues. Lying in bed as long as you possibly can. Lying in the fug of sleep, nightsweat and yesterday's dirty socks. Putting off the evil moment when you have to open your eyes and face the day. When you have to open the curtains and face the boring boredom of another small town day.

Lying in bed till you're so bored with the boring boredom of your own bleeding bedroom that even the unremitting tedium of a Saturday in Greywater, out and about in downtown Greywater, seems a more attractive prospect.

So there's nothing for it but to unstick those sticky eyes, to peel yesterday's smelly socks on to yesterday's sweaty feet because you can't be bothered to find any clean ones. To cover your greasy body with whatever clothes you find at the top of the heap, the heap of clean and dirty all mixed up together because you can never be bothered to sort them, and go out.

You find a stone by the gate and boot it down the hill. You find another stone at the bottom and kick it down Shore Road. You pass Mrs Brown, out walking her boring red setter.

'Morning, Mrs Brown!' you cry, cheerily, and she looks at you, and her red setter looks at you, neither of them responding, neither of them at all convinced by this rare example of friendliness.

You pass Mr Carey, cutting his boring straight line of a boring green hedge.

'Morning, Mr Carey,' you cry, with an enforced air of jollity. 'Lovely hedge!'

And he scowls, knowing you don't mean it. Knowing it for what it is. Teenage sarcasm.

You pass Miss boring Green and Mrs even more boring Fleming, boring the socks off each other on the corner, rabbiting on about last night's blockbuster episode of *EastEnders* or whinging on about all their little aches and pains.

'Morning, Miss Green! Morning Mrs Fleming! Isn't it a lovely day?'

And it isn't. It's grey and there's a chill in the air

and what a big surprise that is and they know you think you're the past-master of postmodern irony and they don't answer, either.

Up on to the railway bridge. Looking up the track, to the tunnel. The long, dark tunnel, beckoning you in. You're bored, but maybe you're not quite that bored. Not quite that desperate for excitement. Not today, anyway.

Down the steps you go, and over to the slipway below the Yacht Club. Jump down on to the beach and scavenge around among the plastic and the sea-weed for some nice round rollable stones. Collect five likely candidates. Place them in a tidy pile at the top of the slipway.

Pick one up. Roll it around in the palm of your hand to test its smoothness, its roundness, its rollability. Swing your arm back. Launch it, underarm, down the slipway, like you're the king of the bowling alley. It rolls and it rolls and just when you think it's going to make it first time, just when you think it's going to reach the sea, it loses its momentum and drops off the edge into the water. None out of one.

You pick up the second. It'd better work this time. You pull back your arm and you launch it down the line. Fast. It rolls and it rolls and it's heading straight down the middle for the incoming wave. The incoming wave that's coming in at exactly the right time. The incoming wave that's going to cut in half the distance the stone has to travel. When suddenly your stone hits a small rock, a rock you hadn't even noticed, a rock that sends it careering off course. Splash, off the side, into the water. Damn. None out of two.

You stomp down to the unseen rock and boot it into the water. Ferociously. You pick up a few straggly bits of seaweed, too. It's cheating, really, to clear the slipway of obstacles. But who cares? No one's watching. And it's your game anyway. You make the rules, so it's up to you whether you want to change them. Or break them. OK?

Back to the top again. You pick up a third little, sweet little, round little stone. If this doesn't work, you're going home. No, if this doesn't work you're not going home. You're going to grab number four. You're going to close your eyes, spin around and around, gaining momentum like one of those Olympic hammer throwers, built like a brick, and you're going to fling it into the air. And if it breaks a

136

window in the boring bloody Yacht Club, or if it cracks the mast of one of their precious bloody boats, well it serves them right for being so damn BORING. So damn rich and so damn boring.

You kiss the sweet little, round little, third little stone and you launch it, straight and fast and right down the middle. Down and down and down it goes, never once veering from the path you've instructed it to take. You're running down after it to will it on, to will it in. Keep going, keep going, keep going. And YES! YES, you did it!

Small pleasures in a small town.

Mountain Madness

Jesse Flood – Aged 14½

It's all too much. Back at school and it's all too much. Riding the train and it's all too much. Charlie dead. My mum gone. Dad trying too hard to sort himself out, to sort me out. A big question mark over my friendship with Flynn. And all I'm doing is waiting, waiting to see what happens next.

It's like I'm swimming. It's like I'm swimming out to sea and my arms are tired and my legs are tired and I'm out of breath and my chest's hurting and it's too far to go back and I don't want to go back, anyway, I want to go forward, I want to keep moving forward. But I need a rock, a rock to rise up out of the waves. Just one rock, to clamber out on, where I can catch my breath, draw in a bit of warmth, regain some strength, before I carry on.

And that's the trouble. There's no rock in my life. No Green Lady to watch over me. There's nowhere restful. Nowhere safe.

I was planning to go into town, to study in the library, but I don't. The sun's shining in a clear mid-winter sky and I stay on the train, for some reason, through to the other side of town, through to the mountains. I get out at a tiny station in the middle of nowhere, and I start walking, up an almost invisible path. It's crazy, I know. I've no food, no proper mountain gear, nothing. And it's winter. Winter, and there's snow on top.

I love it, though. I came here once with Dad. That's how I knew where to get off. What direction to start walking in. It was once only, years ago, but I've always remembered it. The freedom of the mountains, one foot in front of the other, onwards and upwards, higher and higher. And the view at the top. Amazing!

I stop at the lake and throw stones at the frozen water. They slide across the ice, all the way to the other side, and I listen to them singing. Then I pick up some more, one at a time, and fling them high in the air. They come down, crack, on to the ice, puncturing it. Puncturing it but not breaking through, so they stay there, sticking up out of the ice like tiny stranded whales. I try walking along the edge, then, to see if it'll hold me up, but the ice creaks and bends under my weight. Not a good idea, wet feet. Not a good idea at all.

I rummage about at the bottom of my bag and find a bar of chocolate. Delicious, melt in the mouth delicious. It gives me the hit I need to carry on, up the path.

It's warm. Walking this fast, this hard, it's warm. I've got my coat off now and I can feel the sweat on my back. The sun's streaming down from the top of the mountain, but there's a breeze rising up off the frozen lake, chilling the sweat on my back. I strip off my T-shirt and turn it inside out, so the wet bit's at the front, so the sun has a chance to dry it.

I reach the snow-line and I'm glad I'm wearing my boots. I go over to the edge, and I look down at the lake, far below me. I pick up a stone and fling it outwards, fling it with all my might, hoping it'll reach the frozen lake, but it's further than it looks and the stone drops into a gully.

I trudge on, till I reach the first peak. It's colder, up here. Much colder, now I'm in the wind. I put my jumper back on, and then my coat, and I head downwards, to the dip before the final climb. I've got up some speed now, and at one point I choose to go edge-side of a large rock. Suddenly, to my horror, I feel the snow crumbling under my foot. I throw myself in against the rock and cling on, terrified, as the whole piece of ground I was on a second before turns out to be nothing but snow and ice, dropping away, hundreds of feet down the mountain.

I manage to get round to the other side of the rock and calm my breathing, slow my heart rate. And then I carry on. Keeping well back from the edge now.

It's not far to the top. I'm down in the dip, between the two peaks, and then I'm on the final climb. A hands-on job, this one. Grabbing the frozen rock and hauling myself upwards, over the snow-covered scree. Watching where I put my feet so I don't slip. Up, up, and eventually there.

I'm standing on the mound of stones at the summit of the mountain and it's beautiful. I'm on top of the world and I can see for miles and it's still brilliantly clear. Just one small patch of cloud way over to the right. I see the town, way down below me. I see a boat, sailing up the estuary, and I see the train line, glinting in the sun. The train line, back to Greywater.

I go into the shelter, then. I rummage around in my bag again and find a mushed-up two-day-old egg and cucumber sandwich. Yum!

I stay inside for a while, sitting on the bench in the half-light, trying to read the names carved into the wood. All the people that came here over the years. All the ones that had to leave their mark, in order to prove they'd been here.

And when I come out everything's changed. The force of the wind and snow nearly knocks me off my feet. Incredibly, in less than fifteen minutes, the beautiful, crisp winter day has turned into a blizzard and I can see no more than a few feet in front of me. I duck back into the shelter to gather my thoughts, to think what I'm going to do, but I decide there isn't time to wait for the weather to change. I have to get back down before dark. I have to go now.

I search around in my schoolbag and find my woolly hat and gloves. I remember I'd put them in a few weeks ago and forgotten about them. Thank God for that.

I pull my hat down tight over my ears, button up my coat and I head off, along the ridge, aiming to do the circular walk I did with my dad. But soon the path has disappeared. The visibility's so poor you can hardly see the ground you're walking on.

I work my way over to the edge, to look down, in order to get my bearings, and I can see nothing. Nothing at all. I'm confused. I can't work out where I am. I can't work out which way I'm headed.

I decide to go back to the shelter but I sink into deep snow, up to my knees. It takes a lot of effort to pull myself out, and I feel the cramp in my leg, in both legs. I'm not used to this. I don't like it. I carry on to where the shelter's supposed to be, but I can't find it any more. It's gone.

The panic's rising now. I'm cold. My jeans are soaking and my legs are freezing, where they got buried in snow. My hands, my face, my feet are freezing. I go over to the other side of the ridge and suddenly the cloud lifts for a second and I can see a lake, two lakes, below me. But they're too near. And how come there's more than one of them? There was only one on the way up.

I suddenly realize I'm on completely the wrong side of the ridge, going in completely the wrong direction. There's nothing for it but to turn again, to turn back the way I've just been. It doesn't feel right, but maybe that's where the shelter is.

I'm scared, really scared now, but I trudge on, hoping beyond hope that I find it. It's got to be here, it's got to be here somewhere. And at last there it is, looming up out of the mist. Thank God for that. I go in, take off my soggy gloves and blow hot air on my fingers, trying to warm myself up. I look at my watch and it's four o'clock. Four o'clock and the light's fading. If I don't get down quickly I'll be in major trouble. I won't survive a night in the shelter. I never did get myself a mobile phone, like everyone else in the world seems to have. Who'd want to ring me anyway? But I must admit this is one time it'd come in handy. And there's no way Dad'll call out the Mountain Rescue to come looking for me, because he's no idea I'm even up here. He'll probably just think I'm over at Flynn's, and leave the outside light on.

I decide not to try the ridge this time. It's too dangerous. Too easy to lose my way. The path's not as clear and I don't know it very well. I decide to go back down the way I came. It's further and it'll be tough, but at least I'm not likely to get lost. So off I go, down the mountain. Slipping, sliding, blowing on my fingers, kicking at rocks to try and keep my toes awake. Down to the dip, up to the next peak, keeping well back from the edge. It makes the way longer, longer but safer.

And then the main descent. Down, down, past the lake, down, down, forcing those cold cramped-up legs to keep going. Down, down, across the muddy fields to the station.

And for once my luck turns. A train's on its way. I can hear the whistle in the distance, calling out to straying sheep. Off the rails! Off the rails! Too right.

I hold up my hand, to make sure the driver notices me. It's one of those tiny stations where they only stop if they see you. I jump up and down, I scream and wave, and the train grinds to a halt.

Climbing on board, I drip drip drip over a heater. The guard comes to check my ticket and he can hardly believe what a state I'm in. There's no buffet on the train but he brings me a mug of coffee, pours it from his flask. He even offers to give me the money for a meal at Central, but the train's going straight on to Greywater, so I tell him I'll be fine.

Off the train, up the hill and I let myself in.

'Sorry I'm late,' I yell to Dad, who's watching the

football. I squelch upstairs and lock myself in the bathroom. I cling to the radiator, shivering while the bath's filling, and then I plunge into its delicious warmth.

'Why are the stairs all wet, Jesse?' says Dad, knocking on the door a bit later.

'Yeah, sorry. I got caught in the rain.'

'Oh well, I'm off to bed,' he says. 'There's some curry in the microwave, if you want to warm it up.' He never was one for asking a lot of questions, my dad. So he never found out where I'd been. How close I came to not coming back.

Yellow Lily

I lie in bed, and I dream of the last Green Lady, still dancing up on One Tree Hill. She's dancing, weaving in and out of my dreams, and I know who she is. Who she really is. The only woman in my life and she's not in my life. My mother.

We didn't love her enough, me and Dad. We didn't respect her enough. We were like the two older brothers, Dan and Stan, blind to her beauty. Like Dan and Stan, we took her for granted and we eventually paid the price.

Put her out of your mind, Jesse Flood. Push her, force her, out of your mind. Out of your dreams. It doesn't do any good.

She's not a myth. She's not a fairy queen. She's real live flesh and blood and she's gone. Real live flesh and blood and there's no point idolising her. It was her decision, and she's responsible. She could have stayed but she chose to leave. She could have seen it through, for richer for poorer, in sickness or in health, but when it really came down to it, she didn't. She chose to put herself before her duty, before her responsibility to her family. She chose to abandon her husband, abandon her son. She chose to abandon ME.

So how can she try and blame anyone else? She should never have married my father, she should never have had me, if she wasn't going to stay around to see me grow up. To help me in the growing. Selfish, that's all she is. Selfish. Just seeking her own personal happiness at the expense of everyone else. It's all her fault and I don't want to think about her any more.

I lie in bed, and I dream of Sophie Cameron instead. Sophie Cameron, aka Yellow Lily, stepping out of the lake. Her long blonde hair, dripping with water. I'm staring at her hair, staring at the water, and suddenly, to my horror, I realize she's not even wearing that delicious one piece she had on by the pool the other day. No, this time she's naked. Stark staring naked.

And then, from somewhere behind me, somewhere above me, somewhere all around there's a cry, ringing, echoing down the tunnel of memory.

'YELLOW LILY LOVES JESSE FLOOD!'
'YELLOW LILY LOVES JESSE FLOOD!'

The King and Queen of Erin had only one son, and his name was Jesse. Was his name Jesse? Anyway, he was their only son and there was nothing he liked better than to wander the hills from dawn till dusk. Well, one day the ground began to rock, the rocks began to roll, and there in front of him was an Ugly Great Giant.

'Are you any good at cards, young fellow?' said the Giant.

'I am, indeed,' said the King's son.

'Sit down on that boulder, then, and we'll have a wee game.'

So they played for the largest field and the young man won.

The next day they played for five hundred bullocks, and the young man won again.

Well, the third day the Giant said they'd have to play for their heads.

'Sure, isn't my own much bigger than yours,' said he to the prince, 'and I'm not afraid!'

So they played for their heads, and guess what? The Giant won and the prince lost.

'You've four days to say goodbye to the world,' said the Giant. 'And then you must come to my castle.'

The King's son went straight home, plugged in his electric guitar and blasted the night away.

And in the morning he was gone.

He walked and he walked till he came to a tiny cottage. The little old woman who lived there gave him a bed for the night, and in the morning she said, 'I know well the journey you're on, young man. For you've lost your head to the Ugly Great Giant.'

The prince nodded, sadly.

'The Giant has a great castle with seven hundred iron spikes,' continued the woman. 'And on every spike but one is the head of a king's son. The last one's for you, unless you take my advice.'

'I will, I will,' cried the prince, desperately. 'Just tell me what to do!'

'Follow your nose,' said the old woman, 'till you come to the lake of the Giant. There you'll see his daughter, Yellow Lily, on her way down to swim. While she's in the water, slip away with her clothes.'

So the King's son did as he was told. He followed

his nose, all the way to the lake of the Giant, where he hid behind a rock and waited. At midday the girl came down to the lake, and while she was swimming the prince slipped out and stole her clothes, just as he'd been told.

'Whoever took my clothes . . . ' cried Yellow Lily, her eyes searching the silence ' . . . I'll forgive you if you bring them here. And if you're in any danger I'll save you!'

Now, the son of the King of Erin found it hard to believe that a naked girl could save him from an Ugly Great Giant, but he knew he had to take any chance going, so he tossed the clothes out from behind the rock.

'Thank you,' said Yellow Lily, dressing quickly. Then she took him back to the castle and the next morning she brought him to the Giant.

'Come here, boy!' said the big fellow, licking his lips. 'I've a stable out here in which I keep sixty horses, and it hasn't been cleaned these two hundred years. When my great-grandmother was a girl she lost a brooch in there, and she never could find it. You've got till nightfall, and if you don't discover it I'll have your head – on a spike!'

The King's son found an old shovel, and he set to work. But for every shovelful of muck he threw out, two came in again. Don't ask me why – magic, I suppose.

'How are you getting on?' came a voice from outside. It was Yellow Lily.

'Not too well, I'm afraid,' said the prince.

'Hang on a sec,' said Yellow Lily, and she hitched up her skirts and hopped over the stable door. She worked like a demon and within an hour and a half the stable was cleared. And not only that but she held the sparkling brooch in her hand, too.

When the Giant came home his face dropped. 'It's the devil or my daughter that helped you in your work today,' said he, crossly, 'for you could never have done it by yourself!'

'It's neither the devil nor your daughter, but my own strength that did it,' said the Son of the King of Erin, deciding that a little white lie wouldn't go too much against him when his life was at stake.

'Right, boy!' said the Giant, the next morning. 'You're to find the tallest tree in the forest. It's nine hundred feet or more, the only branch on it is a tiny twig at the very top, and resting on that twig there's a crow's nest with one egg in. I want that egg for my supper tonight, or you know what you'll get . . . '

'Head on a spike?' said the prince, grimly.

'Head on a spike!' grinned the Giant.

When the King's son found the tree he did his best to shake the egg out of the nest, but he couldn't. He tried to climb up the trunk, but it was as slippery as a fish.

He was sitting on a stump with his head in his hands, when up came Yellow Lily.

'Saying goodbye to your head?' she joked.

'It's not funny,' said the prince. 'If I can't fetch an egg from the top of that tree I'm a goner.'

'It's a long way up, sure enough,' said the girl, craning her neck. 'Sit down and have something to eat while I think about it.'

'Now, you might not like this idea much,' said she after a while, 'but it's the only way you'll save your head.'

'How's that?' asked the prince.

'You've to kill me,' said Yellow Lily, handing him a knife. 'Strip the flesh from my bones, take them apart, and use them as steps for climbing the tree. Then when you're coming down, collect each bone behind you and put them back together. Drape my flesh over them, sprinkle me with water from this spring, and I'll be alive again and no harm done!'

'You're joking!' said the King's son.

'I'll be fine, believe me,' said the girl, 'for I'm not of your kind. And I'm only doing it because I love you,' she added, kissing him on the lips.

Well, that made all the difference, I can tell you, so the prince took the knife and sharpened it on a stone.

'And don't forget all my bones on the way down,' said Yellow Lily, 'or you won't be able to put me back together again.'

It was a bad business, but the Son of the King of Erin felt he had no choice other than to do as she said. So he killed poor Yellow Lily, cut the flesh from her bones and took them apart. Then, as he went up, he pushed each bone into the side of the tree ahead of him. He used them as steps till he came to the nest.

He picked up the egg and wrapped it safely. Then he tucked it deep into his pocket and down he came, putting his foot on every bone. When he'd used each one he pulled it out and brought it with him, so that by the time he was almost down he had every bone but the bottom one.

With a whoop and a holler he jumped to the ground, laid all Yellow Lily's bones back in the right order by the side of the spring and sprinkled water on them. She rose up before him, just as she'd said she would, but there was a terrible look on her face.

'Didn't I tell you to collect up all my bones on the way down?' she cried.

'That's what I did,' said the prince.

'You did NOT!' cried the girl. 'You left my little toe on the tree, and now I've only nine.'

The young man ran back to the tree and tried to pull out the bottom bone, but it was stuck fast.

'It's no use,' said Yellow Lily, sadly, 'for now I'm lame. You had to do it then and there for it to work.'

When the Giant came home that night he demanded the crow's egg.

'I have it here,' said the Son of the King of Erin, handing it to him.

'Tarnation!' cried the Giant. 'The last spike will have to stay empty for a little while longer, then. 'But I swear you must have had the devil or my daughter on your side!'

'You're right,' said the prince, deciding to risk the truth at last. 'It's Yellow Lily who's been helping me all this time! We love each other, and I'm taking her away with me.'

'Oh no, you're not!' cried the Giant, furiously. 'You've been cheating me, Son of the King of Erin. And you know what I do to cheats?'

The prince didn't hang around to find out. He grabbed Yellow Lily by the hand and together they ran like the wind. Well, they were small and the Giant was big, so they could squeeze through doorways he couldn't fit through, and hide in places he couldn't see. At last they came to the gates of the castle, ran across the drawbridge, and headed off across the open ground.

'We'll be fine,' said the Son of the King of Erin.

'We won't,' said Yellow Lily, stumbling, 'for I'm lame, without my toe-bone, and I can't run a step more.'

The prince picked her up and carried her on his back, but they were too slow.

'He's at the gates of the castle, coming across the drawbridge!' cried the girl, looking back. 'He'll have us in no time!'

And he would have had, too. But what the prince and the girl didn't know was that a trillion woodworm had been slowly eating their way through the great blocks of wood that held the bridge in place. It was strong enough to hold the weight of Yellow Lily and the King's son, but when the Ugly Great Giant came bounding across it, the bridge chose that very moment to collapse into the raging torrents below, taking the Giant with it.

So Yellow Lily married the Son of the King of Erin, and from that day to this there were no more giants in Ireland.

Now that's what I call a story!

But you wake up from dreams to the cold light of day.

Fact / Fiction

A nd yet. And yet.

Sometimes it's hard to tell the difference, even now. Sometimes it's still hard to tell whether you're imagining something or whether it's really happening. It's like the way you remember things from when you were a kid, and you never really question whether they're true or not.

Jesse Flood – Age about 8

I've got this horrible memory of me and Frankie Campbell, round the back of the bus sheds. There's a certain scene that keeps playing and replaying in my head, like I'm being forced to watch some extended action replay on the Big Match highlights, over and over and over. Every time it flashes in front of my eyes I keep hoping it's going to be the last time I see it, but it never is.

We weren't allowed to go there, you see. Round

the back of the bus sheds. It was supposed to be really dangerous, for some reason. But you know what it's like when you're kids, if you're told not to do something then that's what you've just got to do. So we were messing about, like I said, having a laugh, when I suddenly realized everything had gone quiet. No more Frankie. I looked all around and I couldn't see him anywhere and then I heard this faint 'Help!' from somewhere over to my left. I went over to where I thought it was coming from and cried, 'Frankie? Is that you?'

'Help!' he called again, from somewhere below me. 'Get me out of here!'

I stepped back, realizing I was standing on the very edge of a deep, dark, hole. Realizing that Frankie was trapped inside.

And do you know what I did? I ran straight home. Intending, of course, to tell someone. Someone who could do something. But no one was in, and by the time my mum came back with the shopping I didn't know what to say, and I felt so bad about having left Frankie there on his own for so long, and I was scared of what my dad would do if he heard I'd been playing round the back of the sheds when he'd always told me not to. So I said nothing. Not to Mum. Not to Dad. Not ever.

It still haunts me that. My cowardice. Leaving Frankie to drown in a great pool of bus oil. To die of hunger, undiscovered. To be eaten by the creatures of the deep dark underworld. Whatever.

Mind you, he didn't. Didn't die, that is. Someone, a bus driver or someone, must have heard him yelling. Once Frankie realized I'd gone. Once he realized I wasn't coming back.

Yes, someone obviously got him out, because he's alive and well and still kicking around Greywater. But I never hang about with him any more. We live in the same small town still, but our worlds moved apart.

It happens like that. Some leave, like Ed Hawkins. Some stay. Some disappear out of your life, even though they're only round the corner. Some reappear back into it, like Beca. And some come back to haunt you, haunt you in your dreams, like Charlie Ferguson.

But Frankie. Frankie was the disappearing type. We fell out of friendship, went to different schools and that was that.

So I never dared ask him if it really happened, all that falling down a hole stuff, or if it was just a dream.

Just a dream I had. Because I hope, I really hope, it was just a dream. The product of an overactive childhood imagination. But, deep down, at the core of my being, even though Frankie's never come up to me and asked me what the hell I thought I was playing at, deep down, I don't believe it was.

Jesse Flood – Age ?

I used to be able to fly, too, when I was younger. I'd run down the road, pick up speed, and just take off into the air. I'm sure I did. I'd be flying along, past cars and people and houses. And then I'd come back to ground, and everything would be just the same as before. Now how did I do that, I wonder? Did I do that? It seems unlikely, it seems impossible in fact, but it's so firmly stuck in my brain, it's so *actual*, that I can't quite bring myself to completely rule it out.

It doesn't work now of course, that flying business. I try it every now and again just to check – run, pick up speed, leap into the air. But no, I'm back down again before you can say Batman and Robin.
  Maybe it's not that it never happened, though. Maybe it's just that now, now I'm a bit older and

wiser, now that I have a better understanding of the way things work, my body's forgotten how to do it. Now that I've sort of learned the rules of gravity and all that, I have to obey them. That's what I think, anyway. That's what I want to think.

It's like learning to write left-handed. Switching from right to left with barely any effort. I could do it when I was nine, because my brain thought it might help me with my maths. But I know better now. I know the two things aren't really connected. So now I couldn't do it. Couldn't just switch like that. It wouldn't work. Do you see what I mean?

So is it my imagination or is that Yellow Lily, I mean Sophie Cameron, there in front of me. There in front of me with her foot in plaster?

'Oi!' says the ticket man, as I run past him, flashing my train pass. If you don't wear the proper uniform, and I still don't, whatever they say, they always think you're out to cheat the system. That you've mugged some poor schoolkid and you're trying to get away without paying.

'Oi!' cries the conductor as I jump on, just as the doors are closing. They hate you doing that, too.

The train pulls out and I stumble forward, into the carriage. Next thing my foot catches on something and I go flying.

Straight into Sophie Cameron's lap.

'I'm sorry,' I say, recoiling into myself, embarrassed as hell when I see who it is. 'Someone tripped me up.'

I look behind me, to see who stuck out their foot, to give them a piece of my mind. And see a metal crutch, sticking out into the corridor.

'No, it's my fault, Jesse,' says Sophie, smiling. 'I should be more careful where I leave it. I'm just glad it was the crutch and not my foot you kicked.'

And then I notice it, her foot, resting on the seat opposite. It's all wrapped in purple plaster, and my heart stops.

Don't tell me she's lost a toe. A Yellow Lily toe, the one I left in the tree. Because I'm having enough trouble trying to fit into the real world these days. The last thing I need is for the line between fact and fiction to start going all fuzzy on me again.

'What happened?' I say, completely forgetting, in all my *déjà vu* confusion, that I don't talk to girls. Especially girls as pretty as Sophie Cameron. Especially, in fact, Sophie Cameron herself.

'I broke it,' she says. 'Broke my toe, twisted my ankle.'

'Your toe . . . ' I hear myself repeating, like some sort of out-of-sync ventriloquist's dummy. I plump myself down in the seat next to it. Next to her toe, that is. She has to hoick her foot up in the air and move it across to make room for me.

'I'm sorry,' I say again, hearing her groan slightly.

'It's fine,' she says. 'There's lots of room.'

But I can't take my eyes off her foot, off her poor broken toe. It's all I can do to stop myself picking it up, caressing it, telling her it's all my fault, telling my beloved Yellow Lily how desperately sorry I am that I left the last of her bones in the tree. How terrible I feel that I put both our lives at risk by my careless-ness, by my utter stupidity. How overjoyed I am that she and I have been saved from the clutches of the Ugly Great Giant by a trillion ravenous woodworm.

And then I hear a voice from the seat opposite.

'Don't you know it's bad manners to stare at a woman's leg, Jesse Flood?'

It's Beca Douglas, sitting next to Sophie, watching me with that calm, amused, ever-so-grown-up look on her face that she always seems to wear these days. In all my fluster, I hadn't even noticed she was there. In fact, I wasn't even aware there was anyone else in the whole carriage.

'But how, Sophie?' I plead, turning back to the girl of my dreams. 'How did it happen?'

'It's only a toe, Jesse,' Sophie answers, laughing at my seriousness. 'I will survive, you know.'

'Yes, but HOW?' I insist. 'I have to know how you did it.'

'Playing hockey,' says Sophie, raising her eyebrows. 'It's no great mystery. But Jesse, I didn't know you cared.'

'I don't. I do. It's just . . . ' I look around me, panicking. How did I get here? What's happening?

'Yeah, Annie Chambers whacked me with her stick the other day,' Sophie explains. 'It was flipping painful at the time, I can tell you. But we won the match, so that's all right,' she adds with a laugh, 'Beca scored in the last minute.'

She looks over at her friend and then back at me again. That cool, self-confident smile.

And a wave of relief runs through me. A wave of softness. It's only Sophie Cameron. My Sophie Cameron. The girl of my dreams, yes, but not Yellow

Lily. Not the girl of my imagination.

I haven't killed her. She didn't kiss me. There's nobody's head on a spike. Because fact is fact and here and now and fiction is fiction is fiction.

But then I hear the dreaded whistle. Three blasts of the whistle and we're heading into the tunnel. The tunnel of death, the tunnel of love, the tunnel of death, the tunnel of love . . .

Twice in the past year I thought I was going to die in that tunnel. Once from fear, standing in the railman's coffin. And once from embarrassment.

I close my eyes and remember the fear. Did it really happen? Did a train really come? Or was it a myth, a myth of my own making. A story Dominic Flynn, alcohol, passive dodgy smoking, or my overactive imagination had created.

I open my eyes and remember the embarrassment. The moment in the tunnel when I thought I was going to die from shame. The awful moment when I heard Beca Douglas, shouting, 'Sophie Cameron loves Jesse Flood!'

Now what was that, I wonder? Tease or truth? Fact or fiction? I'd always assumed it was fiction, a nasty little out-of-character piece of spite. But what if it wasn't? What if it was real?

I've already made enough of a fool of myself for one day. But I'm here. This is my chance to find out. My chance to separate fact from fiction, dreams from daybreak, once and for all.

Yes, here we are, back in the tunnel. Back in the darkness, back in the noise, and a voice, my voice, rising up from my throat, rising above the roar of the tunnel, words I never thought I'd hear, words I never thought I'd say:

'JESSE FLOOD LOVES SOPHIE CAMERON!'

'JESSE FLOOD LOVES SOPHIE CAMERON!'

And this time I know, beyond a doubt, that I'm not dreaming.

Mad and misguided, maybe, but definitely not dreaming.

Yes!

It's weird, this business of living. This business of being a teenager. I was talking about it to Flynn a while back and he said it's like you're in a tunnel. For years and years you're in a tunnel, a dark, empty tunnel where nothing ever changes. There's nothing before and nothing behind, no way in and no way out, for years. You can't even really breathe properly, and all you can do is wait and wait, gasping for air – waiting for the sun to shine again, waiting for someone to come and show you the way through. Someone to show you who you really are.

And I said, yeah, but other times it's like you're in a completely different sort of tunnel. It's a dark, dark tunnel, like you said, but you're not just stranded there, waiting for the light. No, this time you're racing through it, you're pounding down the tracks like you've got to get to the other end, like there's a tiger on your tail, an engine on your heels, like there's nothing you can do but rush, race, run, towards the thing you're supposed to become.

You're running and running and you think you're coming to the end, you think at last you're coming into the light, into the future, but there's always one more bend. The darkness carries on. And on. And on.

But either way, we agreed, me and Flynn, you're stuck in that tunnel. Stuck in that tunnel for years, the slowest years of your life, with no way of knowing where it's going to lead. No way of knowing when it's going to end, and what you're going to find, and who you're going to be when you come out on the other side. If you ever do come out the other side.

And the only way to get through it, that tunnel, and not just become the exact same as everyone else . . . yes, the only way to stay true to who you really are and not come blinking into the sunlight a carbon copy of all the others – little job, little house, little car, little wifey – is to do things differently. To go slightly off the rails. To go a bit haywire.

It was weird, having that conversation, though. Weird that Flynn brought it up like that. Because I'd never even told him about me and the tunnel. About standing in the middle, waiting for the train. Maybe he knew, though.

Maybe he'd done it too.

Maybe everyone does it.

And the other weird thing is that, even though Flynn's twenty-three or whatever, I get the feeling sometimes that he's still in there, somehow. Still stuck in his own tunnel. Stuck in his own story. He stayed true to himself, OK, but something must have happened. Something must have happened while he was inside. Maybe he got a vision of who he was going to become and didn't like it. Maybe he decided life in the half-light of the tunnel was better than the glare of grown-up reality, grown-up responsibility. Maybe he's still living there, half in the tunnel, half out.

And maybe that's what happened to Charlie Ferguson, too. Except Charlie took it one stage further, and made certain sure he'd never come out.

Yeah, everything about this thing's weird, but the weirdest of all, I mean the strangest, oddest, craziest thing, is that when I get off the train after meeting hopalong Sophie, there's my mum, standing on the station platform. Just standing there, slap bang in front of me. Now how weird is that?

'Hi, Jesse,' she says. 'Remember me?'

I remember you all right. You look a whole heap different, though – new clothes, new hairstyle, a whole new look about you. But you're still my mum. I'm hardly likely to forget you.

She's standing back, smiling a nervous sort of a smile, waiting for me to make the first move. Waiting to see how I'll respond.

And what do I do? I fling my bag in the air and run towards her. I throw my arms around her, laughing and crying all at the same time. And everyone else is standing around watching, like it's some sort of soap opera. Or walking swiftly past, pretending not to notice.

And there's Sophie and Beca, last out of the carriage because of Sophie's leg. Beca sees all my books lying around on the platform and she's picking them up, because she's always been a tidy sort of a person, and I'm shouting, 'Hey, Sophie, Beca, come and see my mum!'

And they do. They come over, like it's the most normal thing in the world. Like it's no big deal the woman's been gone for months. Like they don't even know the whole town's been buzzing with gossip, all about me and my 'dysfunctional' family.

'Hi, Mrs Flood,' says Beca, handing me my bag. And she's smiling at Mum like they've known each other for ever. Like they've both known me for ever. I suppose they have, in a way.

'Hi, Mrs Flood,' says Sophie, smiling too.

And Mum's really nice to them. 'Whatever happened to your leg, Sophie?' she says, all concerned.

And next thing they're chatting away and we're all heading off to the café together. And all four of us are sitting round the table in the milk bar, like real people do. And I'm not just watching, from the outside, like I usually am. No, I'm there. I'm a part of it. I'm behaving like a normal, sociable, human being, surrounded by people I want to be with, people who seem to want to be with me. And it's good. It feels good.

And I don't actually have the slightest idea what's going to happen next. I don't know if Mum's coming back to live with us or if she's not. Probably not, I suppose, because we're talking real life here, not some happy-ever-after fairy tale, but somehow it doesn't seem to matter so much now. Now that I know she's still around. Now that I know we can still be friends.

And I haven't a clue whether there really is something between me and Sophie, either, or whether it's all in my head. I suspect it's just another product of my overactive imagination, even though we're here, barely inches from each other, and she's doing her best to laugh at my feeble jokes. Because how could someone like her, someone who could choose to be with anyone she wanted, possibly want to be with someone like me?

In fact, I don't even know for sure if any of this is really happening, all this milk bar thing, all this 'Hi Jesse, remember me?' thing. All this 'Jesse Flood loves Sophie Cameron' thing. Or if it's just another story, just another dream.

But it doesn't really matter. At this particular moment it doesn't really matter. Because I'm going to enjoy it while it lasts, whatever it is. I'm going to have one more cream cake, one more cup of coffee, one more look around at these bright, smiling, happy faces.

And that'll do. Just for now, Jesse Flood, that'll do.